REBEL HEIR

VI KEELAND
PENELOPE WARD

REBEL HEIR

Editor: Elaine York, Allusion Graphics, LLC
Cover model: Micah Truitt
Photographer: Leonardo Corredor
Cover designer: Sommer Stein, Perfect Pear Creative,
www.perfectpearcreative.com
Proofreading & Formatting: Elaine York, Allusion
Graphics, LLC, www.allusiongraphics.com

REBEL HEIR

CHAPTER 1

Gia

"I've never even *had* sex on the beach, no less *made* one."

"There are two other bartenders. They can help you make whatever you don't know. *Pleeeeaaase.* My sister's water just broke, and I want to drive back to New Jersey tonight to avoid the morning traffic. I'll owe you one." I heard Riley pouting through the phone.

"But I was going to write tonight."

"You didn't come to the beach today because you were going to write all day. How many words have you written so far?"

I looked down at my laptop. *Seven. I wrote seven damn words today.* "More than yesterday." Sadly, that was the truth. "But I'm on a roll."

"*Pretty please.* It's an emergency, or I wouldn't ask."

I huffed, "Fine."

Riley squealed. "*Thank you!* Oh! And wear something low cut to show off that big rack of yours. No one will care if you don't know how to make a drink with those on display."

"Goodbye, Riley."

I looked in the mirror. My dark hair was in a messy bun piled on top of my head. I had no makeup on and already switched out my contacts for glasses that hid my tired, blue eyes. I sighed. At least I'd showered today.

My roommate, Riley, bartended in one of the trendy Hampton bars down by the beach. It was the type of place that snotty, rich, yuppie guys sported polos with little horses embroidered on them and loafers with no socks. The women were all thin and flaunted excessive, perfectly tanned skin. After the last run-in I had with a guy there, I definitely wasn't looking to attract attention. I brushed on some mascara, let my hair down from the bun, and didn't bother to put my contacts back in. *Good enough.*

The parking lot at The Heights was packed. The place had a rooftop bar. Thus, the name. People were smoking out front, and the music from inside blared so loud that the windows vibrated. I remembered from the one time I'd come that there were three bars...the rooftop, one inside, and one outside on the deck that overlooked the beach. There was also an adjacent restaurant that seemed to be popular before the bar crowd took over. I wasn't sure where my roommate was working tonight.

A giant man opened the door as I approached, so I went to check inside first. Riley spotted me right away. Yelling, she waved two hands in the air from behind the bar, then cupped them around her mouth. "Come on back. I'll give you a quick tour." I walked to the end of the long bar and lifted the hinged top for access.

"This is Carly." She pointed to a redhead wearing pigtails and a half-shirt. The woman waved. "She works the outside bar with Michael. Just popped in to steal some of our glasses because she didn't stock her own bar well enough."

Carly shrugged before lifting a box and yelled over the music. "I'm always late."

Riley pointed to a shorter, blonde girl who made Carly's skimpy outfit look matronly. For a second, it made me regret not changing into something a little nicer or at least fixing myself up a bit. "And that is Tia. She works the left half of the inside bar. I work the right."

Tia waved.

Riley drummed her fingernails on the top of a row of taps. "Okay. So we have Bud, Stella, Corona, Heineken, Amstel, and Lighthouse Ale, which is a local brew. Push the local brew if they tell you to pick one."

"Got it." I nodded.

She turned to the mirrored shelves behind us. "Everything is top shelf. The most popular stuff—vodka, Jack Daniels, rum, Fireball, tequila—are all stocked on the left and right side of the bar so we're not banging into each other as much." She pointed to beneath the bar. "Glasses, syrups, sinks, and coolers for bottled beer are all under here. On top of the red cooler, there's a laminated book that gives you the ingredients to any cocktail you don't know how to make."

"Red cooler. Got it."

She tapped her finger to her lip. "What else? *Oh.* If anyone gives you any problems, just whistle, and Oak will take care of it."

"Oak?"

She motioned to the front door manned by the huge man that I'd passed on the way in. "The bouncer. I don't know his real name. Everyone just calls him Oak. I assume it's because he's built like a tree. He's the bouncer and fill-in manager when the owner isn't around." Riley pulled her purse from under the bar and lifted the strap onto her shoulder. "Which, lucky for me and you, he shouldn't be tonight. He'd freak out if he knew I left someone without experience behind the bar."

My eyes widened. "He *shouldn't* be in tonight? What happens if he shows up?"

"Relax. The rich prick was in the City for some board meeting today. He's not going to show up."

Riley kissed my cheek and ran out from behind the door. She yelled over her shoulder, "Thanks for doing this. I owe you one."

My first few customers ordered beer. Aside from some extra foam because I hadn't mastered the art of pouring yet, no one seemed to be the wiser—that is, until a group of four women approached.

"I'll have a Cosmo."

"I'll have a Paloma."

"I'll have a Moscow Mule."

A what?

"I'll take a Corona, please."

At least the one with manners wouldn't be getting her drink screwed up. I poured the Corona, shook up a Cosmo—since it happened to be my favorite, I actually knew how to make that one—and then started to flip

4

through the drink mix book that was on top of the red cooler. Only...it didn't have a recipe for a Moscow Mule or a Paloma. I headed down to Tia.

"Hey...what goes into a Moscow Mule?"

"Seriously? I've never been asked to make one, but I think it's two ounces of vodka, four ounces of ginger beer, and lime juice."

"Thanks. What about a Paloma?"

"Who the hell are you serving?" She laughed. "Two ounces of tequila, seven of grapefruit soda, and lime juice. The weird drink mixers like ginger beer and grapefruit soda are in the bottom of the cooler. You'll have to dig."

"Got it. Thanks."

On my way back down to the other end of the bar, I stopped to refill a beer and made change for someone. The music was just so loud and distracting, and I was feeling a bit overwhelmed, so by the time I grabbed glasses and started to make the ladies' drinks, I wasn't sure I remembered it correctly.

Was it ginger ale, beer, vodka, and lemon? I looked down to the other end of the bar. Tia had a shaker going in one hand and the other was pouring a beer. The bar was also starting to get backed up.

"Did you forget about our drinks?" Mule lover had an attitude.

"Coming right up." *And don't blame me if it tastes like crap.*

I whipped up my best impersonation of the stupid cocktails and poured them both into a fancy glass. Everything tasted better in a swanky glass anyway. After I rang them up, I moved on to the next customer.

"I'll take a mudslide," the guy with the pastel pink polo said.

"Umm. Okay." I glanced down to Tia. She was still busy. I couldn't interrupt her for every customer. "That's with Kahlua, right?"

The guy gave me a look. What was with everyone at this place? "Maybe you should get a job at the ice cream store down the block if you don't know how to make a mudslide."

"Maybe you should drink beer instead of a ladies' drink," I countered.

"It's for my girlfriend. Not that it's any of your business."

"Oh."

I walked to the recipe book. *Why aren't these things in alphabetical order?* Mudslide was second to last. *Vodka, Bailey's Irish Cream, Kahlua, Milk—all in equal parts.*

Two other customers ordered their drinks as I mixed the cocktail. I needed to learn not to make eye contact until I was ready to take the next order. Because of the interruptions, I'd inadvertently put in Bailey's twice and forgotten the milk.

While I rang up snotty mudslide guy's drink, the foursome of women I'd served returned to the bar. They pushed their way to the front and slammed two glasses down on the bar. The liquid from the drinks splashed all over.

"These aren't right. I don't know what you put in them, but they taste terrible."

"Okay. Give me one minute, and I'll remake them for you."

The woman at the forefront of the bitch brigade rolled her eyes.

I took the twenty-dollar bill from mudslide guy over to the register and returned with his five dollars in change. *Fifteen bucks. What a rip off.*

"Here you go."

The guy had a milk mustache as he lowered what I'd just concocted. "This isn't right, either. Do you know what the hell you're even doing back there?"

"*No!*" I yelled back in defense. "I'm helping out a friend. You don't have to be so rude. I'm doing my best."

I took my time remaking all three drinks and had the snooty patrons taste test them this time before walking away. I'd felt someone watching me from the end of the long bar, but had to work my way over.

It wasn't until I'd finished taking care of two more customers that I got a quick look at the eyes I'd felt following me. I did a double take. This guy was gorgeous. *Drop dead gorgeous*, but he also stood out like a pit bull amongst a sea of poodles. Black leather biker jacket, sun-kissed skin, scruff on his face, dirty blond hair that stuck out all over in a messy way that looked like maybe he'd just had sex. *Really good sex.* My eyes caught with his deep green ones, and his intense stare made me nervous. "I'll be right with you."

He nodded once.

After I finished with the guy next to him, I turned my attention to the rebel in the middle of a sea of pastel polo preppies.

"What can I get for you?"

"What do you know how to make?" God, the voice matched his face. Sexy, deep, and intense.

Apparently, he'd been sitting there for a while and figured out I wasn't the best bartender. "Beer," I grinned. "I know how to make beer."

I caught a glimpse of a lip twitch—I thought. "The owner realized when he hired you that you only knew one drink recipe?"

"Actually, he didn't exactly hire me. I'm filling in for a friend, and I honestly don't have a clue what I'm doing. I think I might've even given the last guy the wrong change."

The guy was quiet. He seemed to be studying me, and it made me uneasy. I didn't know many actual badasses, and this guy was clearly a badass.

"So...what can I get for you?"

Rather than answer, he stood and took off his leather jacket. I gulped getting a look at the muscles bulging from the plain white T-shirt he wore. Tattoos covered his arms, coiling around like ivy to cover every inch of skin. I had the craziest urge to examine them up close—ask him what each of them meant.

"What's your name?" He hadn't taken his eyes off of me, yet I didn't really feel like he was checking me out. It was confusing and intriguing at the same time.

"Gia."

"Gia." He repeated after me. "Tell me, *Gia*, what would the owner think if he knew you were behind that bar giving out wrong change and pissing off his customers?"

This guy might've been sexy as hell, but his sudden change in tone had warning bells going off. Yet, I didn't walk away or call Oak. I stood there answering like an idiot. *An idiot who vomited truth when she got nervous.* "I'm thinking the owner would probably be pissed off. He wouldn't see it as me doing a good deed for a friend who had to leave in an emergency."

"And why is that?"

"Well…I heard he's a prick."

He cocked a brow. "Yes. I've met him, and he *is* a prick."

Even though he'd agreed with me, it didn't sound like he was on my side at all. I needed to extricate myself from this bizarre conversation. "So…would you like my specialty…a beer?"

"Sure."

"What kind?"

He shook his head slowly. "You pick."

Relieved to escape for a few minutes, I walked over to the tap, pulled a beer mug from the crate under the counter, and started to fill it with the local beer that Riley had told me to push. Still feeling those eyes on me, I glanced back over my shoulder at my rebel customer and found him staring. He didn't even have the courtesy to pretend he wasn't when I'd caught him.

"That'll be six dollars," I said setting down the full mug.

"Eight."

"Pardon?"

"The beer, it's eight bucks, not six." He seemed a bit annoyed.

"Oh. You're correcting me so you can pay more?"

The bouncer-manager-tree walked up to the bar and stood next to my customer. "Liquor delivery came late and was short four bottles. Receipt is under the cash drawer, boss."

It took a minute for what I'd heard to sink in. My eyes widened. "Did you say...*boss*?"

Badass glared at me. "That's right, Gia. *I'm* the prick. I own this place." His mouth curved into a smile that was anything but happy. "Now, get the fuck out of my bar and tell your friend *she's fired*."

Shit!

He was the boss.

I figured this guy for some kind of drifter passing through town on his bike, not the owner of the entire establishment.

Everyone was staring at me as I scrambled to find the right words.

"You can't do that. You can't fire her. Don't blame Riley because I can't make drinks to save my life. That's not her fault. She was trying to do a good thing by having me step in because of her family emergency. She could have just left you high and dry. Don't punish her for my incompetence."

When the bouncer approached again, the prick held out his hand without breaking his stare, which was firmly directed at me. "Not now, Freddie."

"Sorry, boss. I have to let you know that Elaina just called out. She's not coming back to work at all. Decided to head to the City with her boyfriend. They both got auditions for some play. She said she's really sorry but that she quit."

The prick ran his hands through his hair in frustration and gritted his teeth. "What the fuck?" He looked like he was going to blow. He let out a deep sigh then closed his eyes to compose himself. When he opened them, he just glared at me.

He was so intimidating, but I wasn't about to let him see me sweat. I needed to stand my ground and defend what I knew in my heart was right.

I gave him a few seconds to process the news that had just pissed him off even more and then I pleaded, "Please. You need to reconsider. I'm not leaving until you assure me that Riley hasn't lost her job over this. It's not fair."

He gave me a once-over. "You can't bartend for shit...but can you stand around, look pretty, seat people, and carry the occasional tray of food, if needed?"

"What are you talking about?"

"The nighttime hostess just quit. I'm not going to be able to find someone in time for the Friday night rush, which is about to start rolling in any minute. If you help me out, I'll let your friend, Riley, keep her job."

He wanted to hire me?

"You just tried to kick me out! Now you want me to work here?"

"Yeah, well, I'm in a bind I didn't anticipate, and I had a few minutes to digest your sorry excuse. It seems you had good intentions in helping your friend, even though it was a dumbass move on her part to ask you to do that."

"So, what if I don't accept the job?"

"Then Riley gets fired for putting someone behind my bar who shouldn't have been there. The choice is yours."

It took a moment to really consider his proposal. Or was it extortion? The truth was, I needed the extra money. I'd blown the ten-grand advance I received from the publisher of the book I was writing to rent the summer share I was living in. Getting an extra job that would provide some supplementary income was something I'd been considering anyway. This could actually really work in my favor.

"Is this job offer just for tonight or until you find someone permanent?"

"I don't know. I haven't gotten that far. Are you in or not?"

"I'll take it...but I want the position permanently. And it's not because I'm giving in to your bribery. It's because I'd actually like a job to supplement my income. I'm writing a book, and I blew most of the advance, so..."

He squinted. "You're writing a book? I hope it's not *Bartending for Dummies*?"

"Very funny. No. It's a romance set in a summer house. I'm renting a share house locally for research purposes and currently living beyond my means. The job will actually be very helpful if I can write during the day and work at night."

"A romance in a summer house. Sounds dumb as shit." He took out a cigarette and lit it, blowing some of the smoke toward my face.

I coughed. "Excuse me? Why is that dumb?"

"I don't know much about romance novels, but that sounds cliché as fuck."

Thank you, Mr. Prick, for pointing out the obvious! Cliché. As. Fuck.

How to make it original is precisely my problem.

It started out okay. The first three chapters were good enough to land me the publishing deal. Now nothing was coming out. Thus, the whopping seven words I'd written today.

He flicked some of the ashes on the ground. "By the way, you start in fifteen minutes, Shakespeare."

"My last name is Mirabelli...Gia Mirabelli...for your paperwork purposes."

He blew out more smoke and nudged his head. "Rush."

"I thought you said I had fifteen minutes. Pipe down. I don't need to rush."

He looked up at the sky as if to question the gods as to how I could be so stupid. "Rush is my *name*, genius, and watch your mouth. I'm your boss, remember?"

I don't know where my sass was coming from, but I felt full of it all of a sudden. Straightening my posture, I unleashed it on him. "At this point in time, it seems like you need *me* more than I need you. While this job is going to be helpful to me, I can take it or leave it. So, I say we agree to mutually respect one another. If you disrespect me, I'll tell you to pipe down again." I leaned in. "I'll tell you to fuck off, too."

I braced myself, expecting to get reamed for that. Instead, a wide smile spread over his face like a Cheshire cat. He placed his hand on my arm and led me away from the bar, which was now unmanned. He whispered in my ear, "Save that language for my ears only and watch yourself in front of the customers, please."

That choice of words was odd. *He was encouraging me to swear at him?*

Shivers ran down my spine. The smell of cigarette smoke and cologne invaded my senses. Being this close to him made my body involuntarily react, even though I'd sworn off men after my bad one-night stand gone wrong a couple of weeks ago. But my reaction to Mr. Mean was a reminder that you couldn't exactly choose whom you're physically drawn to. Sometimes, it's the last person you *should* be attracted to.

Clearing my throat, I asked, "How do I get paid?"

"Go freshen up. Do your job, and I'll make sure you're taken care of."

"Is there any formal training?"

He put out his cigarette and blew out the last of the smoke. "No."

"No?"

"No. It's not that difficult." He pointed to the hostess station. "See that standup table over there? You stand there, greet people, and you show them to a table if they opt not to head to one of the bars. If any of the staff has a problem or issue with a customer, they may come to you since you have the least to do out of everyone. Just wing it. It requires no skill, which is a good thing after your failed stint as a bartender. People learn by doing anyway. I'm a big proponent of throwing people into the fire, not wasting time trying to explain things—well, aside from having to drag you away from the bar today when you were losing me customers."

"Sounds like a healthy work environment."

He winked. "Don't forget to smile, Shakespeare."

CHAPTER 2

Rush

I didn't really have a role at The Heights. As owner of the joint, I wasn't required to be here much of the time. That was what a manager and employees were for. But you could say I was a bit of a control freak. Plus, out of all of the businesses I owned, I favored the busy atmosphere of this place. It was where I felt most invigorated. So, I made it my home base.

Tonight, however, I seemed to be favoring The Heights *a lot* more than usual, and it was pissing me off. Every time I would catch myself looking over at my new hire, Gia, I would mentally scold myself. But she was hard not to look at. With long, wild dark hair, an infectious smile, and more spunk than she could contain in that petite frame, she stood out from the moment I'd first laid eyes on her. And she was wearing glasses, which for some reason I found extremely hot.

I didn't live by a lot of rules. For the most part, I did what I wanted regardless of consequences. Smoking was an example. I knew it was terrible for me, but I did it anyway, even though I kept telling myself that I'd quit one day.

Lord knows I had the means to do whatever the hell I wanted in life. That was pretty crazy to be able to say at twenty-nine. The world was at my fingertips, and as a result, it was really easy to get carried away and mess everything up. But I vowed not to waste the opportunity my grandfather had given me a few years ago when he left me half of his estate, which included multiple properties out here in the Hamptons. Even though I didn't live by many rules, I tried not to fuck up royally.

One big rule I *did* have was to not shit where I eat. Or rather, not to *fuck* where I work. Crossing the line with an employee was a hard limit for me. I'd yet to screw anyone I employed. And I wanted to keep it that way. Therefore, the moment I hired Gia Mirabelli was the moment Gia Mirabelli became off-limits.

Not mixing business with pleasure normally wasn't an issue for me. But when that little firecracker ran her mouth off at me earlier, I could have sworn my dick hardened the second the word *fuck* came out of her mouth. No one spoke to me like that, which was precisely why I liked it when she did. Not to mention, *fuck* is a lot prettier sounding of a word when it comes out of the mouth of a beautiful woman.

Word around The Heights was that people seemed to think I was intimidating, particularly those who worked under me. Aside from Freddie, AKA "Oak"— who, let's face it, didn't have to fear anyone because of his size—people seemed to be almost scared of me. But not Gia. Gia had no fucks left to give, and that was just about the most refreshing thing I'd experienced all year. Maybe ever.

During a slow spot in the evening, I'd had her write down all of her personal information for payroll purposes and—what do you know—turns out she lives in one of my properties that was rented out as a summer share. Since I had a management company that handled the tenants, she would have no easy way of knowing I owned it. I made a mental note to spring that piece of news on her when the opportunity was right.

The connection didn't surprise me. I owned a good chunk of real estate in this part of the Hamptons. My estranged father and brother stayed in the City for the most part, managing the family business there. The Hamptons, though, was primarily my territory, at least from an operations standpoint.

While a casual beach bar by day, at night, The Heights turned into more of a club and restaurant with live music on the rooftop. And on this Friday night, it was packed both indoors and outside.

Once again, I found my eyes firmly planted on Gia. She was actually damn good at this job I'd given her. I'd downplayed the role of hostess earlier, but it wasn't as easy as I'd made it out to be. She greeted every customer with a bright and enthusiastic smile, as if they were the very first ones to walk in the door. She also took the initiative to walk around to the tables and check on patrons during the breaks when there wasn't anyone in line. Thankfully, she seemed oblivious to the fact that I was watching her.

By the time everyone cleared out, it was well past midnight. It was starting to rain, and the nearby ocean was getting choppy. I was outside smoking a cigarette when Gia walked right into my cloud of smoke.

"I didn't realize you were still here," she said.

Smoke billowed from my mouth as I said, "Sorry to disappoint you."

"You didn't. I just...figured you'd be gone a long time ago."

"Nice job tonight."

"Whoa." She smiled wide. "Is that a compliment?"

"I call it like I see it. I'd tell you if you sucked, too. While you couldn't bartend to save your life...you were a hell of a hostess."

"With the most-ess." She winked. "Well, I kind of have experience. I used to have a hostess job in the City."

"You can definitely tell it wasn't your first rodeo." My gaze instinctively fell to her heaving breasts, which were straining against the black bra I could see through her sheer white T-shirt. I pried my eyes upward.

Our eyes locked, and suddenly she seemed eager to leave. "Well...have a good night. I'll be here tomorrow on time." When she started to walk past the lot of cars, I realized she didn't have a vehicle; she was walking.

Dressed like that? At night?

I jumped in my Mustang and drove up beside her, rolling down my window. "Isn't it kind of late for you to be walking alone?"

"It's alright. I don't mind walking."

"It's dark, and there aren't many streetlights on the way to your house."

"How do you know where I live?"

That's right. She didn't know I owned her damn house.

"You gave me your address earlier, remember? I know this town like the back of my hand."

"I see." She continued to walk as I drove slowly alongside her.

"I'll drive you home."

"It's fine."

"It's not fine. You're my employee. You worked late on my watch. If something happens to you on your way home because of that, I'd feel partially responsible. And I don't want that on my conscience."

She stopped walking and put her hands on her hips. "Well, I don't have a car at the moment. So, I'm planning to walk home most nights. If you can't drive me every time, then why bother?"

I wasn't going to waste time trying to rationalize with her. "Get the fuck in the car," I demanded.

She didn't argue as she opened the door and looked at me. "Thanks."

The recognition of her scent and the way it was making me feel put me on edge. I couldn't figure out why I was having this kind of reaction to a woman I'd just met. She seemed familiar, even though I knew we'd never crossed paths before today.

I'd fucked around with a lot of women, to the point where I thought I was immune to feeling like this. But there was something different about Gia that I couldn't put my finger on.

This was dangerous.

I needed another cigarette. I took one out and lit it.

"Do you think you could not smoke in here?" she said.

"No. I can't *not* smoke."

Insisting on smoking when she told me not to was definitely a dick move. I should have been more considerate...but with her in this car, I really needed it. I opened the window and made a conscious effort to blow the smoke out and away from her.

"How long have you owned The Heights?"

"My family built it a decade ago. I've been in charge of it for a few years."

"It's a really nice establishment. I'd only been there once before tonight and had a bad experience. I hadn't come back until today."

My head whipped to the side. "What kind of bad experience?"

"Oh...it wasn't the bar itself or anything."

"What was it, then?"

"I met a guy there and it was...well, it didn't end well. I guess I associate The Heights with that experience. I didn't even want to come today at all when Riley begged me."

The thought of someone she met at my business harming her made my blood boil. I slowed down the car and looked over at her. "Did he hurt you?"

"No."

"What happened then?"

Her blatant response surprised me.

"I let him screw me, and he gave me the wrong number after."

Not many things left me speechless. But hearing her say that definitely put me at a loss for words. It didn't make sense how anyone could manage to get this chick in bed and then give her a wrong number.

Her honesty shocked me. How many women would admit that to their boss? Say anything you want to about Gia, but she was real. Maybe that's what drew me to her. Because so much in my life was superficial and fake. This girl seemed like she had nothing to hide.

She covered her face. "God, why did I just tell you that? I vomit the truth sometimes."

"Well, my mother used to say, 'don't apologize for your truths, only your lies'." I glanced over at her. "He was probably married. We get a lot of those city types in the bar, think they can come and fuck around in the Hamptons then go back to their wives in Manhattan like nothing ever happened."

"You know...I think you're right. He was definitely not who he said he was."

I couldn't control the urge to scold her. "You need to be careful. You shouldn't be going home with men you meet in bars."

"I'm not a slut. I hadn't slept with anyone in months before that. I was lonely, in the mood, and figured why not. This guy...he seemed really put together, well-dressed, articulate. It's not like he promised me marriage, but we spent all night talking before I took him back to my place. He even made plans with me for the following weekend. I didn't think he'd give me the wrong phone number. He was charming...had me fooled. If I could take it back, I absolutely would."

I pulled up to her house—my house—a sprawling five-bedroom, shingle-style beach home that now served as a party pad for a bunch of city dwellers looking to escape Manhattan for the summer.

When I shut off the car, she didn't budge.

"I wish I hadn't just told you all that. I don't want you to judge me or think I would do something like that with a customer ever again."

Who the fuck am I to judge? I've fucked up more than my share of times.

"Believe me, judging you for something like that would be the pot calling the kettle black. We all make mistakes," I simply said, lighting another cigarette. I blew the smoke out the window. "I just want you to be careful at The Heights. It's a meet market."

"Oh, I'm quite aware of that. I got hit on all night tonight, too."

I sucked in my jaw. *I know. I was watching and had to stop myself from getting arrested multiple times in my own bar.*

"Anyway..." she said, "How did you know this was my exact house? You didn't even use navigation."

"I told you. I know this area inside out."

She was silent then said, "Can I ask you a question?"

"Depends on the question."

"How did you come to own The Heights? I mean, you're young and..." She hesitated.

"What..."

"I'm not sure how to explain it, but you don't look like what I would have pictured."

"I don't look like I'm going to be showing up at the local chamber of commerce meeting anytime soon?"

She cracked up. "Basically..."

Did I really want to get into this?
Fuck it.

"In answer to your question, I did nothing to earn The Heights or anything else I own except be born the bastard child of a very wealthy man who I can't even stand to be in the same room with. There's nothing impressive about that, being given wealth and not earning it."

"You're on bad terms with your father?"

"If he had his way, I wouldn't even be in his life, let alone share any of his wealth. When my grandfather found out about my existence, which was later confirmed with a DNA test, everything changed. My granddad was an honorable man. He decided I was worthy of all of the same things that my brother—the legitimate child—got. So, I fell into a lot of wealth that I wasn't really ready for or expecting. But that didn't happen until I was in my twenties."

"Wow. So, you didn't grow up rich?"

"No. I grew up in a humble home on Long Island, lived with my mother and grandmother and watched my mom struggle to raise me alone. Barely had a pot to piss in. So, I don't take any of this for granted."

My eyes stayed glued to her legs as she crossed them. I wondered what they would feel like wrapped around my back. A visual of her buck naked beneath me as I hovered over her caused me to suck in the nicotine harder.

"If you're just like one of us then...why is everyone so damn afraid of you, Rush?"

"What makes you think people are afraid of me?"

I knew there was truth in that but wanted to see what she'd say.

"Well, everyone seems to walk on eggshells around you. That was something I noticed tonight."

"It's because they know I don't take any bullshit. They've seen me fire people for goofing off or fraternizing with customers on the job. They know I don't play around. You should take a lesson from them."

"And what's with the permanent scowl? When I served you at the bar earlier, you looked like you were ready to kill someone."

"I was...I was ready to kill *you*. I was pissed at the girl chasing away my customers."

"Yeah, well, it all worked out in the end...didn't it?"

"The verdict is still out."

She smiled in a way that showed me she knew I was bullshitting her. She sensed that she was safe with me, that there was no way I was going to fire her even if she burned The Heights down. That was the truth. The realization of that was fucked-up."

"Why don't you have a car, Gia?"

"I do." She pointed to a parked hump of metal in the driveway. "It's just out of commission at the moment with a flat and in dire need of new brakes."

"Out of commission? It looks like it's disintegrating into the ground."

"Don't remind me." She suddenly opened the door halfway. "Well...thanks for the ride."

A feeling of disappointment was brewing in my chest. That was when I realized how badly I didn't want her to leave. It was also when I realized how long it had been since I'd opened up even a little to anyone. It was unsettling how much I liked being near this girl.

She turned around before leaving, still halfway in the car. "I got the impression that you enjoyed it when I mouthed off to you earlier..."

Fuck yes, I did.

"What makes you say that?"

"Just a feeling." She leaned in, "Fuck you very much for the ride, Rush. Have a good fucking night."

There it was again. She said the work fuck—twice, mind you—and it travelled straight to my cock, which was now twitching.

She was almost to her door when she turned around and shouted, "And for the record, you don't intimidate me at all anymore."

"Why is that?" I yelled out the window.

"Because anyone who has a little angel hanging from their car mirror can't possibly be that bad." She laughed before running the rest of the way to the entrance.

Once she was out of sight, I allowed the smile I'd been fighting to spread across my face as I leaned my head back on the neck rest.

The angel hanging from my rearview mirror used to belong to my grandmother before she died. She used to have it hanging in her Buick for protection until she became too old to drive. My grandmother was the kindest person I'd ever known and held me in much higher esteem than I ever deserved. I could do no wrong in her eyes. The angel was a reminder to try to live up to that, despite the fact that in reality my personality likened me more to the devil.

CHAPTER 3
Rush

The next evening while Gia was at work, I drove to her place and spent three hours fixing her piece of shit Maxima. It took three trips to the auto parts store, but I was finally able to fix her car. She'd said she needed brakes and a new tire. She failed to mention that she rode the brakes for so long that she also needed rotors and new calipers. Turned out to be a bigger task than I'd originally planned, but I knew if she didn't have a car, I'd end up driving her home again most nights, and that would have been dangerous.

This way I could ensure she could get home safely, and my dick could stay safely in my pants.

After fixing her car, I ran some overdue errands and planned to work on the restaurant's books at home for a few hours. But by eleven, I grew antsy and couldn't sit around anymore, so I headed to The Heights. Gia needed a ride home anyway.

On weeknights, the kitchen closed at eleven. By then, hostess duties were pretty much done, even if the waitresses had tables to finish up. I found Gia sitting at the bar talking to her friend Riley who was on the other side. It was the first time that I'd seen Riley since I almost fired her ass, but wound up hiring her friend instead.

Her eyes grew wide as I approached. Gia mustn't have noticed, since she didn't turn around. I sidled up next to her, leaning my forearms on the bar.

"Anyone fucking working around here?"

Riley jumped and started to dry a glass that looked like it was already dry. She definitely seemed nervous. "It just quieted down. We were busy most of the night."

Gia, on the other hand, didn't flinch at my sudden appearance. "You think the sun comes up just to hear you crow, don't you?"

I had to raise my hand to my mouth and pretend to cough in order to cover my smirk. "I'm not paying you to stand around and bullshit."

She turned and faced me without backing up. "That's right. You're not. Because my shift is over. Signed out with the big tree ten minutes ago. I stopped up at the bar to order a drink before I headed home." She pointed her eyes down to the twenty sitting on the bar in front of her. "That makes me a patron right now. And, personally, I don't like the way I'm being treated as a paying customer."

And there my dick goes again. What the fuck was wrong with me that I *liked* when this girl gave me attitude. A slow smile spread across my face. "You can always go to the bar down the block if you don't like the treatment here."

Poor Riley's head bounced back and forth between us so fast, and she started to look a little pale. Her eyes had grown as big as saucers. *That's right. Fear me. Teach your little friend to do the same.*

While Gia and I glared at each other, Riley stuttered an excuse to get the hell away. "Ummm...I, I...someone needs help down there." She pointed to the other end of the bar. "I'll see you in a little bit, Gia."

"Great," Gia frowned. "Now you've scared away the bartender, and I can't even get a drink."

I mumbled a few curses as I walked around behind the bar and grabbed a highball glass from under the counter. Adding ice, I poured some grenadine over it and filled the remainder of the glass with 7-Up before tossing a few maraschino cherries on the top. When I was done, I slid it across the bar to Gia. "Here you go. Your drink. One Shirley Temple."

"I wanted something harder," she said.

I want to give you something harder too.

Gia flashed a devilish smile and then proceeded to dangle a cherry in front of her mouth before sucking it in. Watching those full lips close around that little cherry, her cheeks hollowing as she sucked, was better foreplay than porn. It was a good thing I'd moved behind the bar to hide the growing swell in my pants.

Goddamn it. I'm horny as shit.

I needed to get laid. That was the problem. It had nothing to do with Little Miss Cherry Sucker. Steering my eyes away to avoid watching her finish off the cherry, my gaze innocently landed on her rack. Although my thoughts were anything but innocent. For a little thing, she had great tits. Full, round, more than a mouthful. I had the strongest urge to run around the bar and chase her, to see them bounce up and down—find out if they were real. I laughed out loud at what my staff would have thought watching that shit go down.

Clearly, I was losing my mind.

"What are you laughing at?" Gia squinted.

"Nothing. Nothing at all." I scrubbed two hands over my face and shook my head a few times to snap myself out of it. Then I made a mental note to text one of my hookups after seeing that Gia got home safely. Every summer, there were always a few who were down for a no-strings attached good time. Based on my appearance, women made assumptions. Fucking who they *thought* I was, made them feel like they were saying fuck you to their rich daddies. I needed to stick to those women and keep my mind out of the gutter when it came to my new employee.

"How was the crowd tonight? Anyone give you a hard time?"

"Nothing I couldn't handle."

"How about the writing? Get anything done today, Shakespeare?"

Gia pulled a small notebook out of her purse that hung on the back of the chair. She flipped through a few pages. "How do you like the name Cedric for a male hero?"

I arched a brow. "Is he a heavyset black comedian?"

"No."

"Then it's a stupid name."

She dug a pen out of her pocketbook and drew a slash through a word that I assumed was Cedric.

"What about Elec?"

"What the fuck is an Elec? Is he an electrician or something?"

Another slash.

"Caine?"

"Does he kill his brother Abel in the story?"

Slash.

"Marley."

"Sing reggae?"

Slash.

"Simon?"

"Nerdy dude with glasses who gets beat up a lot?"

Gia sighed.

I swiped the book from her hands and started to read the rest of the list aloud. "Arlin. Aster. Benson. Tile?" I lowered the book and arched a brow. "Seriously? Tile?"

She leaned over the counter and plucked the book back from my hands. "Give me that if you're going to make fun of me. You think it's so easy, then tell me some good names for a hero that are unique and strong."

"Alright. Let me think." I scratched at the scruff on my chin as if I was actually giving it some thought. Gia looked like she was seriously waiting to hear what I'd come up with. *Poor innocent thing.* I snapped my fingers. "Got the perfect name."

"What?" She legit seemed excited.

"Rush. Name your character Rush."

She tossed the book across the bar at me. "You're a jerk."

I laughed as I caught it. "That's not news to you, sweetheart. How the hell did you start this book without even knowing your character's name, anyway?"

"In the beginning he goes by a nickname. But he needs an actual name, too. Her shoulders slumped. "I can't even pick out the names for characters in this book. How am I supposed to write it all in the next two months?"

"You know what I think?"

"I'm afraid to ask..."

"I think you're stressing yourself out. My mom is a painter. She never really made a living out of it, even though she's really good. She waitressed at night to pay the bills, but painting has always been her passion. When I was a kid, she used to paint all day long with a smile on her face. Then she started to sell them for extra money at flea markets and stuff. It got to the point where she would have to produce a certain number by a set date to display them for sale, and she'd get all stressed out and wouldn't be able to paint. You know what she would do?"

"What?"

"She'd take a few days off from painting and we'd go do fun stuff. Like go to the matinee movies—pay for the first movie and then stay all day sneaking into other movies. Or we'd go mini golfing—she kept two little putters and a few balls in the trunk of her car so we didn't have to pay the rental fee."

"Aww. Your mom sounds great."

"She is. But that's not the point. The point is, you need to get your nose out of your fucking book for a few days to clear your head."

"Maybe you're right."

"I'm always right."

Gia rolled her eyes. "Can I at least get a drink before I head home? A real one?"

I lifted my chin. "What do you want, pain in my ass?"

She clapped her hands together and bopped up and down in her chair.

Oh yeah. They're fucking real.

"I'll take a Cosmo."

"Alright." I reached for a martini glass. "One pussy drink coming up."

She scrunched up her nose. "Do you have to say that?"

"What?"

"That word."

I leaned across the bar, getting my face close to hers, then lowered my voice. "You don't like the word *pussy*?"

She covered her mouth. "No. I don't like that word. Almost as much as I don't like the *other* word."

I grinned. "Cunt? You don't like *cunt* either?"

The corners of her mouth were upturned underneath her hand, even though she tried to pretend it offended her. "Yes, that. Don't say that word either."

"Okay." I whipped up a batch of Cosmos and poured one into the fru-fru glass the sugary crap got served in. Sliding it half way over to her side of the bar, I waited until she reached for it and then wrapped my hand firmly around the stem. "Not so fast. There's a fee for this drink."

"Oh. Sorry." She slid the twenty to my side of the bar.

I shook my head. "Nope. Your money is no good here. I have a rule. I don't charge employees for a drink after their shift, or a meal while they're working."

She looked rightly confused. "But you said there was a fee."

I grinned. "There is. You have to say *pussy*."

"What? No!"

"Say it or no drink."

"You're insane."

"Listen, you're writing a romance book, aren't you?"

"Yes. So?"

"Well what are you going to write when they start getting it on... Baby, spread those legs, I'm gonna eat your *vagina*? Cause I got news for you, Shakespeare, there's only one way to inform your woman that you want a taste—and that's *spread those legs, I'm gonna eat your pussy*."

Gia's mouth dropped open. I took that to mean she wanted to hear some more.

"Actually. In some cases, depending on the mood, if it's the foreplay before a little rough fucking maybe, you could probably use *I'm gonna eat your cunt*, too."

"You're a pig."

I shrugged. "I'm not the one whose job is to write about people fucking, sweetheart."

"Just give me my drink."

I grinned and lifted the Cosmo to my lips. The shit tasted awful, but I lied, nonetheless. "Mmmm. It's delicious."

"Give it to me."

I'd love to give it to you.

I cupped my hand to my ear. "What's that? Did you say *pussy*?" I sipped again.

She wanted to be angry, tried her damndest to look pissed off, but the sparkle in her eyes gave her away. "Stop drinking my drink!"

"Say it."

"*Jerk.*"

"Is that any way to talk to your boss?" I took another sip—the damn little glass was half empty even with my baby sips. What did I overcharge for these four-sip things again? Fifteen bucks?

"Is that any way to talk to your employee? With that language? I could probably sue you for sexual harassment."

"You know what I think about people who fight in court over something that could easily be settled by two adults?"

"What?"

I leaned in. "I think they're *pussies.*"

We glared at each other for a few seconds, then both burst out in a fit of laughter. We laughed our asses off, until Riley walked back to our end of the bar. She smiled. "What's so funny?"

Gia snort laughed. "Rush is a pussy!"

I plucked another glass from the rack and filled it to the brim while tears ran down my face. "Here you go, Shakespeare. You've earned it."

Gia didn't give me a hard time about driving her home. That might've been because it was doubtful she could've walked the distance. After only two little Cosmos she was pretty damn tipsy. I realized just how drunk she was when she asked me to stop at the store on the way home.

"Hey...*puuuuusssssssy*..." She hiccupped. "...can you stop at 7-Eleven?"

I looked over at her and laughed. "Sure, my little cunt, I'd be happy to."

We both burst out laughing as she played with the little angel that dangled from my mirror as we drove.

"Where'd you get this?" she asked.

"My grandmother. When she died, my mom told me I could take anything I wanted of hers. Jewelry or whatever." I lifted my chin toward the angel. "That's what I took. She had it hanging in her car. She was the sweetest lady. But cut her off while driving and she'd let out a string of curses that could make a trucker blush. When she calmed down, she'd kiss two fingers and touch the angel." I shrugged. "It just reminds me of her."

"So you get your penchant for foul language from your grandmother, huh?"

I chuckled. "Never thought of it. But maybe I do."

"Huh,"she said, as if she'd just realized something.

I side glanced over at her and back to the road. "What?"

"You're a man."

"I'm glad you noticed." I smirked. "It's probably my lack of a *pussy* that gave it away."

"I meant you're a man, and you talk about your mom so nicely and remember your grandmother so fondly. And yet you don't get along with your dad."

"And..."

"It's the opposite for me. I have no maternal role models. My mother took off when I was two. I don't even remember her really. I never met my grandmother on her side. My dad raised me alone, and his mother lives in Italy, so I only met her a few times when she would come visit. And I don't speak Italian that well, and she doesn't speak English."

"Your mother took off when you were two?" I pulled into the 7-Eleven parking lot and parked.

"Yep. I found a letter she wrote to my dad saying she was missing the maternal gene and wasn't cut out to be a mother. She had packed a bag and took off. Never heard from her again."

"Shit. That's worse than my asshole of a father."

She sighed. "Parents." Opening the car door, she asked, "You want anything? I'll just be two minutes."

"No. I'm good. Thanks."

A few minutes later she came back to the car. I was curious what we'd stopped for, but figured it might be tampons or something so I didn't ask. Although my curiosity was satisfied when she opened the brown paper bag and whipped out a huge bag of Swedish fish. She tore the thing open like she was starving.

"That's what we stopped for? Candy?"

"What else do you go to 7-Eleven for at midnight?" she said.

"Umm. You go for tampons, condoms, or beer. That's what a midnight 7-Eleven run is for."

She shoved the bag toward me. "Fish?"

"No thanks. I don't eat candy."

"*What?*" She said it like I just admitted I'd killed someone.

"I'm not into sweets. I don't even know how you drink that Cosmo crap. Taste like pure sugar to me."

She tore a fish's head off with her teeth. "That's what makes it so delicious."

I shrugged, staring at her teeth. *I bet they'd feel fucking awesome sinking into my flesh.* Clearing my throat, I diverted my eyes back to driving and backed out of the parking spot. "To each his own. Just not my thing."

She pulled another fish from the bag and waved it at me while she spoke with her mouth full. "What's your thing?"

"My thing?"

"Yeah. Everyone has a vice. I eat sweets when I'm happy or sad. What do you do?"

"Not sure I have a vice that goes with happy or sad, but I smoke more when I'm pissed off." I also liked to fuck *hard*, when I felt rage—which was usually when I was forced to be anywhere in the vicinity of my father. But I decided to leave the latter off, considering Gia was my employee.

"You should really give that up. It's so bad for your health."

"So is candy. You gonna give that up?"

"Maybe...maybe we should get a little bet going to see who can give up their vice longer."

I pulled up in front of her house—*my house*—and put it in park, but left the engine idling. "Oh yeah. What would the bet be for? What do I win?"

Gia tapped her finger to her lips. "Hmmm. I don't know. Let me give it some thought."

I rested one arm on top of the steering wheel. "You do that."

She opened the car door but turned back before getting out. "Thank you for the ride home. Those two drinks went right to my head, and I'm not sure walking would've been a good idea. But don't worry, I'm hoping to get my car back on the road really soon, so you won't have to drive me." She shook her head. "I'm not saying that I would have driven myself home after two drinks. I'd never drink and drive. I actually don't drink often. But you know what I mean. Right? Don't you?"

Being a bar owner, most drunken babbling annoyed the crap out of me, but on Gia, for some reason I found it fucking adorable. "Yes, Gia. I know what you mean."

"Okay, then. *Anywho*. Thanks again."

She started to get out of the car and then I remembered I hadn't told her about fixing her car.

"Wait. I...a..." It hadn't felt odd when I'd fixed it. In fact, it felt just the opposite—like I was *supposed to be* fixing it. Yet now that I was about to tell her what I'd done, I realized for the first time that what *was* odd was my feeling like I was supposed to fix her damn car.

Gia tilted her head waiting for me to finish. A light breeze passed through the open car door, and a wisp of hair blew across her nose. Without thinking, I reached over and brushed it from her face.

Were her lips that fucking plump five minutes ago?

While I stared they parted and her tongue peeked out to trace the length of her bottom lip. The rise and fall of her chest seemed to expand as the inside of my car closed in around us.

Fuck.

It took every ounce of willpower, but I pulled out of whatever the fuck spell she had me falling under. "I gotta get going."

Gia blinked a few times. "Oh. Okay." She started to get out of the car again, and I started to feel like I could breathe. But before she closed the door, she leaned down and showed me her dimples. "You know, you can pretend all you want, but I know you wanted to kiss me just now. You shouldn't have been *a pussy* and just done it." Then she shut the door and yelled, "Good night, bossman."

CHAPTER 4

Gia

The next two days I didn't have to work at the restaurant. Yesterday I'd spent the entire day attempting to write. I'd literally sat at my laptop for twelve hours—and produced nothing. I'd write a few hundred words, read them back, hate every single one of them, and delete. Wash, Rinse, Repeat. By the end of the day, I had added the sum total of nineteen words. Basically, I'd described the sky. I wasn't even sure what the hell all my characters were named yet.

So on the second day of being off, I decided to take Rush's advice and blow off the entire day in an attempt to clear my head. I spent the morning and early part of the afternoon in our beautiful yard, lying by the in-ground pool, working on my tan. After I'd gotten enough sun, I decided to go to the theatre that played foreign films a few towns over. I thought it might be a nice change of pace to spend the day reading subtitles and listening to something in French. But I had no transportation.

I knocked on Riley's bedroom door.

"Come in."

It looked like she might be getting dressed for work. "Are you working at the restaurant today?"

"Yeah. I'm covering Michael's shift. Why, what's up?"

"Do you think I can borrow your car? I'll drop you off at work and then pick you up at the end of your shift?"

She shrugged. "Sure. Are you going anywhere good?"

"I'm going to go the movies by myself."

Riley shook her head. "How many times did you get asked out in the last week working at The Heights? You don't need to go the movies alone."

"All of the guys who come into that place are jerks."

She looked at me in the reflection of the mirror as she tied her hair into a ponytail. "You can't let one bad egg ruin the entire summer for you." I'd confided in Riley about my night with Harlan, the pretty boy I'd slept with who left me with the wrong number.

If I were being honest with myself, I might be letting the sour taste Harlan had left me with taint my thoughts on men who looked like him. But the entire male population out in the Hamptons seemed to be cloned Ken dolls. They looked alike, spoke alike—I'd even noticed most of them *smelled* the same. Well, except one. Rush smelled like something woodsy and cigarette smoke half the time. My thoughts started to drift off to the weird exchange in the car two nights ago. It was as if Riley read my mind.

Finishing her hair, she turned to face me. "What was going on between you and Rush the other night?

One minute he's going to fire both of us and the next the two of you are laughing hysterically and cursing at each other."

"Nothing. He's just fun to screw with."

Her eyebrows jumped. "Rush? Fun? Maybe you spent too much time out by the pool today and heat stroke is making you delirious."

I laughed. "He's got a hard exterior, yes. But I think once you get to know him, there's a decent guy underneath. I like his dry sarcasm and hard wit."

Riley grinned. "Not me. I think once you get past that hard exterior, there's more asshole underneath. Like an onion, every layer you peel back is just more onion. That being said, I bet he fucks like a champ. All that pent-up anger...that *hard* body. He might be an asshole, but he's ridiculously hot."

Well, we could agree on one thing at least... "What time do you have to leave for work? I'd like to take a quick shower if I have time."

She looked at her phone. "I'm working five to midnight. So you have twenty minutes to get yourself all prettied up for your big solo movie outing."

―――――

After seeing two movies, one in French and the other in Italian, I actually felt invigorated. The first film had been about a woman who pretended to be her sister, after her sister died. The film itself was sort of bleak, but it sparked something creative in me. I actually sat in the theatre for a half-hour after the movie ended and typed a boatload of notes into my phone—all ideas for my book.

On the ride over to The Heights to pick up Riley at the end of her shift, I couldn't stop the wheels in my head from spinning. My book started to play out in my imagination like a movie. For the first time, I saw the faces of my characters, felt their movements, and heard their dialogue in my head. It was as if a door that had been locked had magically opened, and I could finally see inside.

I was excited to share my good news with Rush since he'd been the one to suggest stepping away from my work for a day. Only, when I approached the bar, that excitement faded when I found Rush sitting at the bar with a woman. She threw her perfectly coifed head back and laughed at something he said. An unexpected lump formed in my throat. I wanted to turn around, walk back to the car, and send Riley a text to let her know I'd be waiting outside. But before I could do that, Riley yelled my name and waved. Rush's head turned and his eyes landed right on me. I couldn't back out the door gracefully now. I wasn't even sure what the hell was going on with me, why I was feeling the way I did.

I forced a practiced smile and went to the bar.

"Just give me five minutes," Riley yelled from the cash register. "I need to take my drawer into the back to count out and then I can go."

Rush shook his head and mumbled as Riley walked away, "She announces that she's going in the back with a drawer full of cash. I'll be right back. Let me get Oak to keep an eye on the office so she's safe." He stood and looked between me and the woman sitting next to him. "Shakespeare, this is Lauren. Lauren, Shakespeare. She works here when she's not home procrastinating about writing the next great American porn novel."

Rush disappeared and awkwardness set in, at least for me it did. I smiled at the woman, and upon getting a closer look I thoroughly regretted my choice of comfy clothes and piling my hair on top of my head. Because Lauren was beautiful. Her thick blonde hair had that beachy, wavy look that she probably paid a fortune for in a salon, and she wore a baby blue, strapless summer dress which accentuated her sun-kissed skin that, unlike mine, didn't have any tan lines.

She seemed to be studying me. "So...you work here?"

"Yep."

"And you're a writer?"

"Yep."

"Rush mentioned he'd hired a new hostess. In fact, he mentioned you a few times in the hour we've been sitting here."

The woman smiled at me. But it wasn't in the typical I-want-to-claw-your-eyes-out jealous woman kind of way. Of course, that made me assume that Rush had spent the last hour amusing her with stories about me that made me look like an idiot.

"Don't believe anything he says about me. I'm really not a bad employee."

She smiled some more and tilted her head. "He had nothing but nice things to say about you. That's...unlike Rush."

"Umm. Okay. Thanks. I guess?"

Rush walked back over. He looked at me. "Your friend is an airhead. Not only did she announce she was taking the drawer to the office. When I went back to check on her, she had the door wide open and her back to it. I'd fire her ass if I didn't think I'd have to listen to you bitch about it for a month."

My hands went to my hips. "I don't bitch at you."

The woman stood and wrapped her hand around Rush's bicep. "I should be going. I don't want my husband to know I was here."

Rush nodded. "Come on, I'll walk you out." He looked at me. "Be back in a few."

My mouth was still hanging open when he came back to the bar a few minutes later. It wasn't my place, but I couldn't help myself.

"You know, I'm really disappointed in you."

He pulled his head back with the audacity to look surprised. "Me? What the hell did I do?"

"After the way your mother was treated by your father. How could you?"

"What *the fuck* are you talking about?"

"Lauren. She's married! You can have any woman you want." I waved my hand up and down in front of him. "You're gorgeous, got that stupid, hot, bad-boy thing going on that women love, and to top it off, you have money, but don't act like it. Why in the world do you need to go out with a married woman?"

A sly grin spread across his face. "You think I'm hot."

"*That's* what you took out of what I just said?"

Rush leaned down so he was eye level with me, his nose practically touching mine. "Lauren is definitely a married woman. But she's *my half-brother's wife*, not my fucking date."

"I don't...wait...what did you say?"

He scowled. "My *brother's* wife."

"But why would she be here? I thought you and your brother didn't get along?"

"We don't. That's why she stopped in. She's trying to talk me into coming to some ridiculous thirtieth birthday party she's throwing for him. I don't like my brother, but his wife is a nice lady. Although I have no clue why she's married to that asshole."

"Oh."

"Yeah. *Oh*." Rush mimicked me.

I had to admit, the relief I felt upon realizing that Rush wasn't hooking up with her was a little disconcerting.

I thought he was about to go off on me for making assumptions and jumping to the wrong conclusion, but instead he smiled again. "So. You think I'm hot..."

"Forget I ever said that."

"Sorry. Too late." He offered a sly smile and pointed to his head. "Ingrained in here now."

"Great."

Rush leaned into the bar, balancing his body on his strong, tattooed forearms. "What brings you by here on a non-work night? You miss me that much?"

He was so close that I could smell his delicious, woodsy, smoky scent. It literally made me weak.

"Sorry to burst your bubble, but I'm returning Riley's car. I borrowed it for the day. But actually, I did want to thank you."

"For what?"

"Well, I took your advice and went to see a couple of movies to clear my head—like you said your mother used to do. Totally got the creative juices flowing."

"Well, I'm always happy to get your juices flowing."

I could feel my face heat up. "*Creative* juices."

He winked. "Right."

Riley came around the corner, looking eager to leave. "You ready to go?"

Rush answered for me, "Gia's gonna stay for a drink. I'll drive her home."

I turned to him. "You're so bossy. Who says I want to stay for a drink?" Despite giving him lip, I handed her the keys. "Go ahead without me."

She looked skeptically between Rush and me. "Okaaay. Suit yourself. See ya."

Once we were alone, I said, "What's the catch, Rush? What do I have to say to earn my free drink tonight?"

He took a daiquiri glass out from under the counter and slammed it down on the wooden bar top. "The word of the night is cock."

I shook my head. "Original."

Rush poured and mixed a concoction then presented me with a red drink I'd never seen before. He'd even added a cherry and a little purple umbrella.

"What is it?"

He slid it closer to me. "It's a French Kiss."

"What does that have in it?"

"Vodka, raspberry liqueur, Gran Marnier and dash of whipped cream."

I took a sip. It was really good. "Mmm. Thank you very much for this *cock*tail."

"Ah!" He laughed. "That was weak, but I set myself up for that one."

"Still counts."

His eyes followed my every move as I sucked on the maraschino cherry. Something told me that act was partly why he loved serving me drinks. And considering I liked driving Rush crazy, I made sure to do it in slow motion.

Rush swallowed hard. "So, you enjoyed the movie?"

"Movies plural. I saw two. Actually, they were foreign films, one French and one Italian."

"You should have hit me up. I would've gone with you."

Playing with my straw, I said, "I didn't figure you for a foreign film kind of guy."

"T'as de beaux yeux, tu sais?"

Oh my God. Did he just speak French? He was too damn sexy as it was, then to speak the language of love on top of everything else.

"Well, well...what do you know. You speak French?"

"My mother is originally from Canada. She only moved to Long Island as a teenager. She spoke French to me growing up, and I picked up a lot."

"What did you just say to me?"

He smirked teasingly. "I'm not telling you."

"Well, now I'm sorry I didn't ask you to go to the movies. You wouldn't have even needed the subtitles. Anyway, I figured you were working."

He wiped the table. "You're forgetting I'm the boss. I can take off as much time as I want."

"I would've liked the company, but if I'd asked you to the movies, that might have come across as a bit forward, don't you think? I wouldn't have wanted you to take it the wrong way."

Rush paused, then said, "It wouldn't have been a date. I don't date my employees. So, you don't have to worry about me thinking that." He stared at me for a few seconds before he resumed wiping the table.

Well, alright then. Thanks for clarifying that.

I broke the several seconds of silence. "Then why are you even interested in going to the movies with me?"

"Because I sort of like your company."

"Sort of?"

"When you're not pissing me off the other half of the time, yeah."

I laughed. "You don't date your employees. You just order them around and entice them to talk dirty to you."

He shook his head and flashed a naughty grin. "No... just you. You're the only one I want to hear talk dirty."

"Lucky me. You *do* realize that your behavior is odd."

"I never claimed to be normal. You don't know the half of it, Shakespeare." He slapped the hand towel against the bar and swung it over his shoulder. "Anyway, you like hanging out with me, too. Admit it. You could've gone home with Riley. You chose to stick around."

"Actually, if my memory serves me correctly, you *made* that decision for me."

Before he could respond, a tall brunette approached. When Rush's eyes landed on her, he seemed to tense up. She waved and was headed straight toward him.

Wearing a tight, leather half-jacket over a short, white sundress, she was definitely attractive. I was beginning to feel the same way I had when I'd first spotted Lauren earlier.

Here we go again.

"Rush...you're still here," she said. "I was hoping to catch you."

His jaw tensed. "Rachel..."

She glanced over at me and then back at him. "I was just driving by, figured I'd stop in and see if you were still here, see if you'd want to hang out tonight."

He scratched his chin and hesitated. "I have some things to do tonight."

Rachel looked over at me. "Who's this?"

"One of my employees."

I offered my name. "Gia."

Without responding to me, she nudged her head toward the door. "Can we talk for a minute?"

Rush looked pissed but followed her over to a corner where I could still hear what they were saying.

"I miss fucking you, Rush. How come you haven't returned my calls?"

My heart dropped as I continued to eavesdrop.

"Lower your voice," he scolded.

Rush then led her toward the entrance where they lingered for a few minutes. I could no longer hear them, but could see she was running her fingers through his hair. Even though he looked annoyed, it irked me to see her touching him. I had no right to feel that way.

Shake it off, Gia.

After she finally left, he returned to where I was sitting at the bar. He didn't acknowledge what had just happened as he continued to wipe the bar top when there was nothing left to wipe.

"So, who's Rachel?"

"No one," he was quick to say.

"I have ears, you know."

"And what exactly did you hear with those ears, Minnie Mouse?"

"That she misses fucking you. Is she one of your whores?"

He stopped wiping and whipped the towel at me. "Now, now...have some respect. I think the correct term is concubine."

I snapped my fingers. "Ah, sorry. Didn't mean to cheapen it."

He shrugged. "Honestly...she's no one important... just someone I used to mess around with."

"Used to?"

"When I meet someone, I'm very clear on the fact that I don't want a relationship. I don't make any promises. Sometimes women expect things to keep going when they were never meant to go on. Sometimes, no matter how clear you make your intentions, they still don't listen."

"I assume that means you're done with her?"

"There's no reason to continue."

"But she *misses fucking you*," I mocked.

"That's her problem."

"Well, if you really are that upfront with women, then I respect that. I would have preferred it if Harlan—

the guy I met here, if that's even his name—told me that all he was interested in was having sex and running."

Rush lifted his brow. "Would you have fucked him if he'd admitted that?"

"Probably not, but I would've appreciated the brutal honesty over what he did to me."

"He could sense that you aren't the type of girl to go for a one-night stand. He knew the only way to get you to sleep with him was to deceive you into thinking it was the start of something more."

"How do you know that about me...that I'm not the one-night stand type?"

"Well, for one, you told me you were hurt by what happened. If you were different, you wouldn't have given a shit—wouldn't have even thought to tell me about it when you'd only just met me. And even if you hadn't said anything, I would still be able to read you. I can look a woman in the eyes and know if there's a lot going on in her head or if things come up empty. Don't ask me how I know...I just do."

"And you go for the empty ones..."

"Empty is safe."

I pondered why Rush was so intent on distancing himself from relationships. "Do you worry about women only being interested in your money...trying to go after you if things go wrong? Is that why you're the way you are?"

"No. That's not really something I worry about."

"You don't worry about it because you never let things get to a certain point with anyone."

"Pretty much." He grabbed my empty glass and lifted it in the air. "You want another?"

"Do I have to say cock again?"

"You just did."

I laughed. "No more French Kisses for me. Not fake ones anyway." I winked. "Honestly, I have to write tonight while the ideas from today are fresh in my head. I'll pass out if I have any more alcohol. My characters have a lot to say and do."

He chuckled. "Well, at least someone's getting laid tonight."

CHAPTER 5

Rush

Oak snuck up beside me during the evening rush. He was so big that his body cast a shadow whenever he was near.

"You alright, boss?"

Looking up at his massive frame, I said, "Yeah. Why?"

"Well, you seem preoccupied lately. Anything you want to tell me?"

"Not particularly. Why are you asking me that?"

"You don't know why?"

"No, I don't."

He laughed to himself then said, "Pretty sure you have a thing for Gia."

Fuck.

Was it that obvious?

"Are you out of your mind? You know I don't date employees." I looked around to make sure no one was listening to our conversation. "What makes you say that anyway?"

"Oh, I don't know. Ever since she started working here, you never leave The Heights? You also watch her like a hawk when you think no one's looking. But I'm always watching *you*, so that's how I know."

"Well, you can stop watching me. Your job is to watch The Heights, not me."

"My job is to observe *everything*. Part of my job is to protect you."

"Well, I don't need protecting."

"She seems like a nice girl, very sweet to everyone. The customers love her. I think—"

"Save it, Oak. Nothing is going to be happening there."

"It's *already* happening from what I can see..."

Looking up at him, I said, "You're crossing the line. Are you forgetting I could fire your ass?"

His deep laughter filled the ear. "Nah. You won't. I know too much shit."

"That and you're gigantic. I would be fucked. Anyway, you're lucky I like you."

His laughter died down. "Come on, Rush. You can't fool me. You got a thing for Gia. There's nothing wrong with that, man."

"There's plenty wrong with it. First off, she's my employee. Nothing will be happening for that reason alone, but more than that...she's dangerous."

Oak squinted. "Dangerous? That little thing? How do you figure that?"

How was I going to explain this?

"You ever just look at someone and know that if you let them, they could turn your life upside down... completely ruin you?"

Nodding in understanding, he said, "Oh, yes. That's happened to me before."

"What did you do?"

"I gave in and married her."

Hearing him say that freaked me the fuck out.

"Well, that's not happening with Gia—or anyone."

"So, what...you're just gonna continue to guard over her and never tell her how you feel?"

"That's right. My feelings are irrelevant. I can't date an employee and if that weren't an issue, it's not like I can be with anyone who expects anything from me anyway."

"At some point, you're gonna regret being so closed-off. The bad-boy thing ain't gonna be so hot when you're my age and all alone."

I let out a deep sigh. My eyes were on Gia when I said, "She writes romance novels, Oak. Fucking fairytales. That means, deep down, she wants the fairytale for herself. And I'm *not* the fairytale. I'm the horror story. I'm the fucked-up bastard child of an asshole, and it's very likely that the apple doesn't fall far from the tree. I've never been interested in a relationship, and that's not gonna change just because I'm temporarily fixated on her ass, and every other body part."

He just continued to stare at me as if he didn't believe me.

I continued, "I don't know what I'm doing, alright? It's like I want to...protect her or something. It's weird."

He patted me on the back. "As long as you recognize that, boss."

My car was idling as I waited outside for her to exit The Heights. It was sort of an unspoken thing that I'd drive Gia home after her shift. I still hadn't figured out how to tell her I'd fixed her car. Tonight she just started walking right past me even though I knew she damn well saw me.

As I drove alongside her, she joked, "We really have to stop meeting like this."

"Get in."

Gia kept on strolling. "I'm thinking I'd like to walk tonight."

"Not safe."

She started to skip, her wild, black hair blowing in the night wind. "I think I'll risk it."

I could tell by the look on her face that she was messing with me.

"Get your ass in the car, Gia."

She laughed, then opened the car door and situated herself in the passenger seat.

Lighting up a cigarette, I blew the smoke out of the window. "Stubborn little shit," I grumbled, putting the car in drive and speeding away too fast. This was a prime example of taking my sexual tension out on my Mustang. It had been taking a beating lately.

Sucking in another puff, I looked over at her. "Did you get any writing done last night?"

"Yeah, more than usual, but not as much as I'd hoped. I wanted to finish the fourth chapter, and I didn't quite get there."

"What happens if you can't produce this book in time?"

"Then, I'm screwed. I'd have to give the ten-thousand-dollar advance back, which I've already spent, and I could end up being in breach of contract."

"How did you get yourself into this mess?"

"Well, for a lot of people, landing a deal with a big five publishing house is a dream—hardly a mess. In my case, I won a contest based on submitting the first three chapters of the book, which remain the only completed chapters. Once I won, it was like my creativity shut off. It sucks."

"What did you do before you were an author?"

She laughed. "You ready for this?"

"Uh-oh."

Based on her warning, ideas were floating through my mind. *Stripper?* She certainly had the body for it.

As if she read my mind, she said, "It's not that bad or crazy."

"What was it?"

"Well, you know when you pick up a greeting card? The cheesy little saying inside? That was me. I wrote them."

"No kidding?"

"Yeah. I worked for a card company for a few years, writing sweet sentiments."

"I actually think that's pretty cool."

"You know what was really sucky? Having to write Mother's Day cards. That really blew."

Given that Gia's mother had taken off when she was little, that hurt me to hear her say.

"Well, I'm sure you rocked it, even though it was hard."

"Yeah. I tried."

"Why did you leave that job?"

"Well, I got the book deal and decided to write full time. Clearly, I couldn't afford to do that. I was struggling until this bossy, tatted man told me to look pretty and gave me a job."

"Glad to help."

When she kicked her toned legs up on my dash, I nearly swerved off the road. Gia grabbed onto my arm for a split second after practically falling over in her seat.

"So," she said. "What did you do before you became a rebellious heir to a vast fortune?"

"I was a jack of all trades. I worked on cars...I waited tables. I was a tattoo artist for a while and—"

"Really? Can you tattoo something on me? I was thinking of getting one on my lower back with this saying abou—"

"No. That won't be happening."

She narrowed her eyes. "Why no—"

"Gia. Drop it."

When she could see I was serious, she shrugged. "Okay...suit yourself, grumpy."

The ride was quiet until she asked, "Go on, finish telling me about what you used to do. Tattoo artist... what else?"

"It didn't matter what I was doing. I always worked hard, still do...it's just that making actual money is a lot easier now. But like I've said before, I don't take any of it for granted."

"I know you don't." She paused. "How did you find out about your father initially?"

I let out a long breath. What was this girl doing to me? She was getting me to open up, and I didn't like it one bit.

I finally caved and answered her question. "My mother had kept his identity a secret from me for years. Despite his money, she wanted nothing to do with him because of the way he treated her. But she got to a point where she felt I should know who my father was. And I think a part of her felt like I deserved a piece of the pie, even if it sickened her. I could've cared less about the money. In fact, some days, I wish it didn't exist so I wouldn't have to deal with them. The money...the businesses...they're the only things that connect us."

"How did your parents meet?"

"My father was living a double life. He was married when he started dating my mother, picked her up in the diner she was waitressing at. He'd come out to Long Island to see her but never brought her back to the City for fear of being seen. Once she found out the truth, that was the end of it. But by that time, it was too late. She was pregnant with me and eventually found out what a rich, lying prick she'd been involved with."

"You mentioned before that your grandfather was the one who actually saw to it that you got an inheritance?"

"Yes. My grandfather controlled everything at the time. My mother actually went to him without my knowing and told him about me. I was in my teens at the time. She didn't ask for anything, just wanted him to know about my existence. I guess he understood what a loser his own son was. After the DNA test, Grandad had his will redrawn so that I got an equal share of everything when I turned twenty-four. As you can imagine, Daddy Dearest and big brother were just thrilled about that."

"Your grandfather sounds like a good man."

I took a deep breath as memories of him flashed through my mind. "He was. He passed away a couple of years ago. As much as some days I wish I never knew about my history, I'll always be grateful to him and for the brief time I got to know him. Before he died, he always made an effort to visit me to make sure I was doing okay."

When I pulled up to the house, we lingered for a bit until she turned to me.

"Do you want to come in?"

Yes.

"No."

"Why not?"

"You know why."

"I thought you made it clear to me that nothing could ever happen between us."

"Exactly."

"So...what's the harm in coming inside if we know where things stand? Besides, we'll be far from alone."

That was true. She lived with a fuck ton of people in a share house. That made me feel better, and also gave me no real excuse not to take her up on her offer. *Just a few minutes*, I told myself.

I exhaled before shutting off the car and getting out.

It was a beautiful estate—if I did say so myself, right on the water and sprawling. Everything was new inside from top to bottom.

Two girls and a guy were hanging out in the living room watching TV when we entered. Several pizza boxes, beer bottles, and rolled-up napkins were strewn about.

Gia introduced me. "Rush, this is Caroline, Simone, and Allan...three of my roommates." She looked over at me. "This is Rush."

Your landlord. I laughed inwardly.

"Hi," I said, sizing up the dude. I was pretty sure I'd seen him around town before canoodling with another dude.

At least, he was one guy I didn't have to worry about.

I never understood how people could deal with the share house situation. I would never want to live with so many strangers up my ass all of the time. But I knew that for many, that arrangement was the only chance in hell they had of living in the Hamptons for the summer. I hated that I was starting to get a little jaded about that kind of thing, forgetting what it was like to be piss poor.

Gia nudged her head for me to follow her. I had secretly hoped she planned to stay in the main living area.

"Where are we going?"

"To my room..."

The warning bells in my head were officially sounding off. Heading to Gia's bedroom was a bad fucking idea. Not to mention, walking right behind her gave me a view of her ass in the tight black pants she was wearing. My dick stiffened. The only reason I was agreeing to this was to prove a point, that I wasn't afraid to be alone with her.

"Welcome to my humble room." She bounced on the bed. "I lucked out, ended up getting my own bedroom when most of the others have to share."

I looked around at the mostly lavender decor. "It's nice."

She continued to bounce as she looked up at me. Her fucking tits were bouncing right along with her. "You look tense, Rush."

Fiddling with my watch, I said, "It's late."

Gia tilted her head. "Have you given any thought to our bet?"

"Bet?"

"You know...I give up candy and you give up smoking."

That's right.

"Sure, yeah."

Her eyes widened as she leaned in. "And?"

"Why are we bothering with this bet again?"

"We're trying to save your life and save me from diabetes."

"Oh. Gotcha. So, how does it work?" I asked.

"You stop smoking cold turkey, and I stop eating candy. Then we have to come up with penalties if we aren't able to stick to the program."

I had a light bulb moment. I'd been putting off telling her I'd fixed her car because I didn't want her to question my intentions. This was the perfect opportunity to have her indirectly find out about it.

"How about if I lose, I'll fix your car."

Her eyes lit up. "Oh my God. That would be awesome! Is it sad that I might be hoping you slip and fall off the wagon?" She grinned.

"What do I get for holding up my end of the deal?" I asked.

"What's something you want?"

Your lips wrapped tight around my cock.

"I know!" She said. "If I lose, I'll name the main male character in my book Rush."

I bent my head back in laughter. It didn't matter what she planned to give me because I planned on intentionally losing. "We have a deal, then."

"Cool. It starts effective immediately," she said.

Her eyes followed me as I started to wander around her room. Her closet was open. Running my fingers along the hanging outfits, I noticed a set of eyes looking back at me from atop the shelf. Then, another set of eyes. And another.

Lined up in a row were a set of the ugliest dolls I had ever seen in my life. Their hair was all messed up, and some of them looked downright deformed.

"What the fuck do you have going on in here?"

She couldn't stop laughing. "That's my ugly doll collection."

"Ugly is an understatement. These are hideous! Like they give Chucky some serious competition. You collect these?"

"Yup. Don't ask me how I started...because the answer is more fucked-up than the dolls themselves."

"Okay, well, now you know I have to ask. How *did* you start collecting them?"

She sighed, gearing up to tell me a story. "Before my mother took off on my dad and me...she left with me with a parting gift. It was a little doll. It wasn't an ugly doll or anything...it was generic—blonde hair, pink dress. Her name was Lulu. Anyway...when I got old enough to realize that she was never coming back...I burned it...like literally took it out to the backyard when my father was burning wood and threw it into the fire."

"Holy shit."

"Yeah. Well, I immediately had second thoughts. After all, this was the only keepsake I had of my mother. So, I ended up pulling it out a few seconds later. It was all charred and half burnt, but still somewhat recognizable. I liked her better imperfect. She reflected how I felt. When my father figured out what I'd done, he was trying to make me feel better about it. The next day, when he came home from work, he brought home the ugliest doll you've ever seen in your life, because he said Lulu needed a friend. That was the moment I realized I had the best dad in the world. And that was the moment I fell in love with ugly dolls."

I immediately spotted the doll she referred to as Lulu and lifted it. "This is the burnt one, isn't it?"

"Yup. And after that day, I started collecting bizarre looking dolls. They go everywhere with me."

If I didn't already dig this chick, she had to go and tell me she threw a baby doll into a fire. Something about that whole twisted story just warmed my black heart.

"That is one fucked-up story...but kind of fucking awesome at the same time."

"That's the story of my life, Rush." She walked over to me until she was dangerously close.

Fuck, I wanted to kiss her.

Instead, I just walked toward the door and said, "T'as de beaux yeux, tu sais."

"Speaking French again, are we?" She smiled.

"You wanted to know what it meant. It means, *you have beautiful eyes, you know.*"

Gia blushed, and it was fucking adorable. "Thank you."

That was my cue to leave. "I'd better go. See you tomorrow."

She didn't argue with me as I slipped out the door, through the living room, and sped away in my Mustang.

That night, visions of ugly dolls danced in my head. And even though I planned to intentionally lose the bet, I didn't touch another cigarette.

CHAPTER 6

Rush

I *will not go to The Heights.*

I paced back and forth, alone in my living room.

I will not go to The Heights.

More pacing.

I wasn't quite sure which addiction had me unable to sit still tonight. It was now almost twenty-four hours since I'd smoked a cigarette and a half-hour more than that since I'd seen Gia. One made me feel like I was dangling on the edge.

It had to be the cigarettes. I wasn't even sure why the fuck I hadn't smoked today when my plan had been to lose the stupid bet. For some reason, I wanted to see if I could stop if I wanted to. The thought that I'd rather take a ride over to The Heights than smoke really pissed me off.

Flopping down on my couch, I grabbed my cell phone. What I needed was *not* a damn smoke or Gia—I needed to get laid. I scrolled through my contacts to see if any names sparked an interest.

Amy. Redhead. Killer curves. Liked to hang around The Heights and try to distract me. The last thing I needed was another distraction at work.

Blair. Into some weird, kinky shit. Not that I minded, but that type of thing needs a certain mood that I just wasn't feeling today.

Chelsea. Saw her around town last week holding hands with some preppy-looking dude. I didn't have many rules in life, except I don't touch what belongs to someone else. *Delete.*

Darryl. Texted me Memorial Day and said she wouldn't be out until August this year. I couldn't hold out that long.

Everly. Damn. *Everly.*

If anyone could help me take my mind off of things, it was that woman. Best head I'd ever had in my life. We'd been together a few times last summer, and she'd messaged me a few weeks ago to tell me she was back in town. The best part of being with Everly was that she made *me* feel used. She'd tell me exactly what she wanted and how she wanted it, and after we were done—she'd get up, get dressed, and peck my cheek before saying *Thanks. See ya around.*

Perfect. Just what I needed.

My finger hovered over her name while I debated hitting her up. After a few minutes, I tossed my phone on the couch. *What the fuck is wrong with me*? I was acting like Everly was some foul-tasting medicine I had to take in order to get over the flu. When in fact, there was nothing wrong with me.

Stop acting like such a pussy.

Before I could overthink it anymore, I picked up my phone again and shot off a quick text. Why not leave it up to fate? Who knows, maybe she'd met someone and wouldn't be down for a hookup anymore.

Rush: Hey

I had to laugh at myself after hitting send. *Great opening line. Took you ten minutes of debating to come up with that shit. Smooth, Rush. Real smooth.*

Less than a minute later, my phone buzzed with a response.

Everly: Your place or mine.

Fuck. My head fell back against the couch. Guess fate thinks I need to get laid, too. At least it would keep my mouth off Gia and mind off a cigarette. Wait. No. That should be my mouth off a cigarette and mind off of Gia. *Or maybe not.*

I dragged two hands through my hair, then took a deep breath and exhaled loudly before saying *fuck it.*

Rush: Yours.

Everly was basically the female version of me. The old me anyway. Blunt, to the point, and treated sex as mutual pleasure exchanged between two bodies. Emotions weren't part of it.

The dots jumped around while she typed back.

Everly: Be here in an hour...or I start without you.

I scrubbed my hands over my face and decided I wouldn't spend any more time feeling guilty. There was *no reason* to feel guilty. Gia was an employee, and maybe a friend in a loose sense of the word. I didn't owe her celibacy just because I liked to look at her ass and drive her home. Fuck that.

Even though I knew I wasn't doing anything wrong, I couldn't shake the odd, angry feeling I had. That feeling continued while I made myself something to eat and started to get ready to go to Everly's place. Normally, I liked to blast music while I showered, but tonight I was so off that I hadn't remembered to turn the tunes on. Which was why I was able to hear my phone ringing from the other room.

The first time I ignored it.

The second time, I hopped out of the shower and wrapped a towel around my waist while cursing.

"What?" I barked into the phone. Water dripped all over the floor from my soaking wet hair.

"Boss. It's Oak."

"Whatever it is, deal with it. I'm not on tonight. I'm going out."

"But it's Gia, Rush."

Jesus Christ. Could we all just pretend that she didn't exist for tonight so I can go get laid in peace. *"Just deal with whatever it is."*

"Boss..."

"Deal with it!"

I was just about to hang up when he spoke again. "She got hurt, boss. Stepped into the middle of a fight that broke out at the bar. Thought you'd want to know."

My heart felt like it started to ricochet against my ribcage. "Where is she? Is she alright?"

"She'll be fine. She's sitting in the office. But she took a good pop to the eye. Probably gonna have a shiner."

"I'll be right there."

Even Oak looked nervous when he saw my face. Steam might have been coming out my ears with how hot my temper was running. I stalked directly to the office, ignoring anyone who attempted to speak to me.

Gia jumped from the chair when I swung open the door. Something fell to the floor as her hand flew to her chest.

"You scared the crap out of me, Rush!"

I walked over and lifted her chin. Her left eye was puffy and already starting to turn purple underneath. "What the fuck happened? Are you hurt anywhere else?"

She shook her head. "No. I'm fine. Just my eye. It's not a big deal. Oak made me sit back here and put ice on it. But I'm fine. I can go back to work."

Realizing what had dropped when I walked in and startled her, I knelt down and grabbed the ice pack. "You're sure nothing else hurts?"

"I'm positive."

"How *the hell* did this happen?"

Even though I'd seen for myself that she was okay, my heart was still beating at a murderous rate. The sound of blood swishing around in my eardrums made it difficult to hear.

"I was upstairs..." Gia started to say.

"Not you," I cut her off and turned toward the open door. "Oak!" I yelled.

He must've been standing near the door waiting. "Yeah, boss."

I closed my eyes and took a deep breath, trying to remain calm. But the only image I saw when I shut them was of a fist coming at Gia's sweet face. Someone was going to pay for this. And at the moment, it was the man I employed to make sure this type of crap doesn't go down in my bar. "How *the fuck* did this happen?" I roared.

The giant man took one look at my face and actually took a step back. *Smart move.*

"I didn't see it go down. I was downstairs, and it happened on the rooftop, near the bar. Two guys got into it over one buying the other's girl a drink. Gia had gone upstairs to bring a bottle of Patrón up because they were running low. She tried to break up the fight, got in between the two guys."

I heard nothing after the first sentence. "You didn't *see it happen*? Isn't that what I pay you for? To have eyes on this place?"

Oak hung his head. "I'm sorry. It's my fault. I should have been there."

Gia piped in. "This isn't his fault."

"Shut up, Gia. Let me handle this."

My focus had been on Oak, but I caught Gia's eyes go wide out of my peripheral view. She slammed the bag of ice down on the desk in order to free up both hands to fly to her hips.

"*Shut up?* Did you just tell me to *shut up*?"

"Gia...

"Don't Gia me. You can't just march in here and start screaming at Oak and tell me to shut up."

I lowered my head so that our faces were level. I was just about to yell, remind her that it's *my bar* and *my employees*, so I had every fucking right to march anywhere I want and tell off whomever the fuck I wanted. But then I saw her eye again. An ache in my chest reminded me I needed to go easy.

I turned to Oak. "Get out. Shut the door behind you."

He didn't need to be told twice.

Once it was just Gia and me in the small office, I took a few deep breaths and focused on what was important. Cupping her cheeks, I asked, "You sure you're okay?"

Her face softened along with her tone. "I'm fine. Really."

I gently ran my thumb along the bottom of her eye that had started to swell. She winced.

"Did you fall?"

"No. I just stumbled back. I tried to grab one of the guy's arms to stop him from hitting the other one, and an elbow hit me in the eye."

"Rookie move." I examined her eye closer. "You never grab the arm of the guy in a fight."

"What should I have done?"

I locked eyes with her. "*You* should have done nothing. Oak should have gotten the guy in a choke hold or stepped between the two."

"But Oak wasn't there."

I shook my head. I *would* be dealing with that later. But right now, I needed to make sure this was only a black eye. "Any double vision?"

"No."

"Follow my finger." I moved my pointer back and forth to test her eye movement.

"Headache?"

"No."

"Any bleeding before I got here? From the nose or anything?"

"No."

I let out a deep breath. "I think you're going to be fine. You'll have a nice black eye by morning. But ice will keep it from swelling shut." I grabbed the ice pack from the desk. "Keep this on. Come on, I'll drive you home."

While Gia went to grab her purse, I spoke to Oak and found out that both of the assholes who had gotten into the fight had left with black eyes from my bouncer. That was the least he could do.

As soon as Gia and I got outside, I lit a cigarette. The thick smoke coated the burn in my throat like a salve.

"Hey. You're smoking!"

I eyed her. "Fucking A, I am. Your fault."

"My fault? How is it my fault?"

"You scared the shit out of me. Do me a favor. From now on, you see a fight going on, walk in the other direction."

She smiled from ear to ear.

"What the fuck are you smiling at?"

"You care about me. It's sweet that you got scared."

I grumbled and pitched the half-smoked cigarette to the ground. As my eyes lowered to step it out, they snagged on Gia's rack. She had on a sheer blouse, and her nipples were protruding through the fabric. I had the strongest urge to bite them, take out all my pent-up anger and frustration on sucking those things until they were sore as hell. My eyes rose up to meet hers. "I'm not sweet. Trust me."

Unexpectedly, Gia threw her arms around my neck and hugged me. Her tits and those pebbled buds pressed up against my chest. It felt damn good. The blood still rushing through my ears, headed south. She kissed me on the cheek before stepping back.

"What was that for?"

"A lot of things. For being a big old softie under that hardass exterior you wear. For coming to make sure I was okay. Because you're going to fix my car since you lost the bet. And...for stopping at 7-Eleven on the way home so I can pick up some victory candy."

I shook my head and chuckled. "Let's go, Rocky."

———

Gia flopped down on her bed. "Will you lie next to me for a while?"

"That's not a good idea."

She pouted. "But my eye really hurts."

My lip twitched. "You're full of shit and trying to play on my sympathy. I'm not picking up what you're putting down."

She grinned at being called out. "You're not cashing what I'm checking?"

I shook my head. "Not itching what you're scratching."

"Not hitting what I'm pitching?"

I handed her the ice I'd carried in with me. "Put this back on for fifteen. And, no, I'm not rocking what you're rolling."

Her smile was fucking adorable. I walked over to the ugly doll closet and plucked the original one from the shelf. The left side of its face was charred where her eye had been. Same side as Gia's blooming black eye. I set it down beside her on the bed. "Now you look like twins."

My phone vibrated in my pocket. It had done the same on the drive over to Gia's, too. It wasn't until this second time that I realized it was probably Everly. I'd been the one to initiate contact and then stood her up.

Gia pointed her eyes to my pants pocket. "Aren't you going to answer that?"

"No. Not right now."

She assessed me for a minute, and then tilted her head. "It's a woman?"

"I didn't look, so how could I know that?"

She squinted. "It's a woman, isn't it? A late-night booty call."

I looked down at my feet. "I had plans for tonight, yes."

"Oh. I see...." The hurt in her voice killed me. "Then you should probably get going. I wouldn't want to keep you from a good time."

My head, the one attached to my shoulders, screamed *take the cue...run!* But for some godforsaken reason, what I found myself saying was just the opposite. "Move over."

Her face lit up, and she tossed ugly doll on the floor as she inched over and turned on her side.

My brows rose. "Is that any way to treat your prized doll?"

She patted the bed next to her. "It's not like I can make her look any worse."

Knowing it was a bad idea, but doing it anyway, I lay down on the bed next to her. I stared up at the ceiling, tense.

Gia seemed way more comfortable than I was. She moved closer and lifted her head onto my chest.

"I can hear your heartbeat. It sounds like it's going so fast."

That's because it is. I felt like the big bad wolf lying in Little Red Riding Hood's bed, and I really wanted to eat her.

I glanced down at her just as her big eyes looked up at me.

My what big eyes you have,
The kind that drive wolves mad.

She smiled innocently and snuggled closer. Her firm breasts pushed up against my side.

My what big tits you have,
They're sure to lure someone bad.

She yawned. "I'm so tired suddenly."

Without thinking, I reached down and stroked her hair. It felt so natural and right. "Your adrenaline is crashing. It spiked when you jumped into that fight and even for a while after."

She sighed. "Yeah. I'm sorry for doing that. I just sort of did it and didn't think. I'm also sorry for ruining your plans for the night."

"It's fine. They weren't important."

A few minutes later, I heard her breaths change, and I thought she'd fallen asleep. Until I heard her groggy voice. "Rush?"

"Yeah?"

"I'm not really sorry I ruined your plans for the night."

I smiled. "I'm not sorry they got ruined either, Shakespeare. Now get some sleep."

CHAPTER 7

Gia

I woke to an empty bed.

Confused, I wasn't entirely sure if I had imagined the entire night before. I *had* fallen asleep using Rush's chest as a pillow, hadn't I?

Lifting my head, it pounded as I padded to the bathroom. After a quick morning pee, I washed my hands and made the mistake of looking at myself in the mirror.

I grimaced seeing my reflection. My eye had shaded a lovely purplish black, and the top lid had swollen so much that it covered half my eye. I touched a pink lump near my cheekbone. "*Ouch*. Shit."

Luckily, I didn't have to work today, so I decided to get back into bed. A few minutes after I'd shut my eyes, I started to drift off again when I heard a noise. Looking up, I found Rush next to my bed, rustling inside of a bag.

"What are you doing?"

"Sorry. Didn't mean to wake you so early. I'd planned on going to the store before I went home. But we both fell asleep last night."

I lifted up onto one elbow. "What is all that?"

"Went to the drugstore to pick you up some supplies."

"Supplies?"

"For your shiner." He held up a bottle of Motrin and a bottle of Vitamin C before placing both on the nightstand next to my bed. "Motrin for the headache you probably have this morning. Vitamin C to strengthen the blood vessels and speed up the healing of a black eye." Reaching in the bag he pulled out a plastic container of...*are those pineapples?*

"Pineapples have enzymes that reduce inflammation and accelerate healing," he said.

"Really?"

"Yep." He pulled the last item out of the plastic bag. It looked like a piece of blue terry cloth material with something stuffed inside. "Warm compresses on day two and three. This gets microwaved until it's warm. Not hot."

"Okay." I laughed. "How do you know so much about this stuff?"

"Got into my share of fights growing up."

"Oh."

He leaned down and kissed my forehead. "Gotta get going. You're off today, right?"

"Yes."

"Good. Get some rest. I have to head into the City."

"For what?"

"Some stupid board meeting for a company I own part of. My grandfather left me a shit load of shares with voting rights. I could do an absentee ballot, or not vote at all, but it upsets my dear old dad and brother when I attend. So, I make it my business to show up to every fucking one."

I laughed. "I'd like to be a fly on that wall."

"Take it easy today." Rush tapped the tip of my nose with his pointer and turned to leave. He'd stayed the entire night, yet I still didn't want him to go.

"Wait!" I pulled the covers back.

"Your board meeting is in Manhattan, right?"

"Yes."

"Whereabouts?"

"My father's office is on Madison Avenue."

"Oh that's funny. That's where my literary agent is. Are you taking the train, or driving?"

"Driving. It's a pain in the ass, but the meeting isn't until one, so I'll wait until after the morning rush hour passes."

"Can I hitch a ride with you?"

His brows drew down. "To the City? You want to come to the board meeting?"

"No. My dad works there. I haven't seen him in a while, so it would be fun to surprise him and take him out to lunch."

Rush shrugged. "Sure. As long as you don't touch my radio or bitch about my smoking."

I leapt out of bed, forgetting all about my headache and achy eye. "What time should I be ready?"

"Ten. I'm going to run some errands before I go home and shower. I'll swing by and get you before I hop on the road."

"Okay!"

"Did you bring something to change into?" I glanced over my shoulder into the backseat of Rush's car. There wasn't a garment bag or any suit hanging.

"You don't like what I'm wearing?"

If I was being honest, I loved what he had on. Ripped jeans, black, high-laced, military-style boots, a white T-shirt and a leather jacket. It was as if James Dean came back to life, only hotter and tatted. "I like the style. But it's not exactly appropriate for a board meeting, is it?"

A mischievous smile spread across Rush's face. "Nope. Not at all."

"Will your father say something to you? Make a scene because of the way you're dressed?"

"I'd respect him more if he did. He's only ever judged me for who he thinks I am. Never bothered to get to know me."

"Well, then, it's his loss. Because I, for one, happen to know that underneath that rebel exterior is a man who won't let his brand-new employee walk home, even if she did screw up half the drinks she'd made for customers and pissed him off."

"Thanks. But I think you see the best in people. And because of that, sometimes you miss part of the equation."

"What are you talking about?"

"You think I drove you home because I'm a good person. I'm not so sure that's the case. If I'm being honest, I think what you look like probably had something to do with my being a decent guy and offering you a ride."

"I don't believe that for a minute. I think you'd offer any employee a ride home. You just don't *want* people to know that about you. Besides, you barely even noticed what I looked like the night we met and you drove me home."

Rush lit a cigarette and sucked in a long drag of smoke. Blowing it out the window, he turned to me. "White T-shirt with a V-neck that laced up, black bra underneath. Denim jeans with a rip in one knee. The left, to be specific. Hair down, loose and wavy. Glasses."

My mouth dropped open. He'd just perfectly described what I wore the night we met, down to the bra I hadn't even realized was visible under my shirt.

Rush glanced over and caught the surprise on my face. "Glasses were sexy as shit, by the way. You should wear them more often."

I laughed. "I think you have a really good memory, and your motives were more altruistic than you want me to believe."

He puffed his cigarette. "Suit yourself. But I'm showing you a wolf and yet you still want to see me as the sheep."

Rush's cell rang. Glancing at the name flashing, he said it was a liquor distributor he'd been trying to reach and he had to take it. Of course, he broke the rules of the road and spoke holding the cell to his ear instead of on hands-free. I looked out the window while he argued with someone over how many cases of vodka were delivered.

We'd just merged onto the Long Island Expressway and had another two hours of drive time in front of us.

When I'd asked Rush this morning if I could hop a ride with him to the city, it was mostly a ploy to spend more time with him. But now that it was getting closer to surprising my dad for lunch, I was really excited about it. It had been at least two months since I'd seen him. We talked on the phone every few days, but we normally didn't go this long without spending time together.

When Rush hung up, I was still thinking about my father. I said, "When I was a kid, my dad and I used to take a road trip every summer."

He tossed his cell on the dashboard. "Oh yeah? Where'd you go?"

I shrugged. "Nowhere fancy. We didn't have a lot of money, but Dad always made sure we got a vacation in. Sometimes it was Pennsylvania, sometimes Maine. A few times we even drove down to Florida. We used to play car games the entire trip. I'm not even sure if they were real games, or if Dad made them up."

"What? Like the license plate game where you have to find all the states."

"No. They were always games where we had to make up stories and stuff. My favorite was *fortunately-unfortunately*."

Rush glanced over at me and back to the road. "Never heard of it."

"One person would say something fortunate that starts with *Fortunately* and then the next person would have to make up something unfortunate about the previous situation. If you stumble giving the unfortunate story to go with the fortunate story, you get a strike. Three strikes and the other person wins."

"I don't get it."

"Like this..." I tapped my finger to my lip and stared out the window as we drove until I thought of something. "*Fortunately,* Rush was going into the City today, and I could hitch a ride. Now you have to come up with the next part, relating to my part, and your sentence has to start with Unfortunately. Go ahead. Give it a try. I'll say mine again. *Fortunately,* Rush was going into the City today, and I could hitch a ride."

Rush grinned as he continued to keep his eyes on the road. "Unfortunately, Gia remembered this stupid fucking game and ruined the ride into the City."

"That's it! That's how it goes. Except you're a jerk."

Rush chuckled.

"I'm starting over now that you got the hang of it." I smiled. "Fortunately, Rush missed his date last night, which meant he was spared a hideous case of the crabs."

He shook his head. "Unfortunately, he now had blue balls and will be needing to borrow the icepack that Gia used after her barroom brawl last night."

I kept it going. "Fortunately, Rush has a strong right hand and can take care of that problem easier than clearing up an STD."

"Unfortunately, Rush's dick knows the difference between beating off and being inside a woman."

I laughed. "You're really good at this! In a twisted sort of way."

"Oh yeah? Just wait. On the way home I'm going to start all the stories. And I've got nothing better to do than sit in my board meeting all day and think of warped shit for you to have to answer later."

Why was I sort of looking forward to that?

As we continued to drive, it dawned on me that I'd been spending all of this time with Rush and didn't even know his last name.

I turned to him. "Hey...I never asked, what's your last name?"

His jaw tensed. "That's kind of a random question..."

"Yeah, well, I just realized it's a little weird that I don't know."

He let out a harsh breath. "You don't need to know my last name."

"You slept in my bed last night. I think the least you could do is tell me your last name. Besides, it's not like I couldn't just ask someone at work what it is."

"Actually, the only one who knows is Oak. And he's been given strict instructions not to give it out to anyone—that includes you, Gia Mirabelli."

"Oh my God. That's so shady." I laughed. "Why?"

"Because people don't need to know my fucking business."

"It's your *name*! That's hardly private information."

"It is to me."

I leaned in a little. My voice was low and sexy. "Come on. Tell me."

"No," he spewed.

"Why?"

Silence.

More silence.

He wasn't even answering me anymore. I was becoming more and more curious by the second. I devised a plan that I hoped would work.

When I started to wave at the driver of a big rig next to us, he yelled, "What the hell are you doing?"

"If you don't tell me your name, I'm gonna flash that trucker."

The driver honked at me and smiled. I really wasn't going to go through with it, but Rush had no way of knowing that.

His Mustang swerved a little. "You wouldn't do that..."

My eyes widened. "Oh yeah? Watch me."

A vein in his neck popped as I began to lift my shirt. Either he was going to tell me his last name, or he was going to crash the car. Just as the material was almost all the way up, Rush blurted it out.

"My name is Heathcliff Rushmore!" He expended a breath and grumbled, "Fuck."

Heathcliff Rushmore?

Heathcliff?

Rushmore?

I covered my mouth. "Oh my...that's interesting."

He looked so angry at himself. "Happy now?"

I beamed. "Yes, actually, I am." I repeated to myself, "Heathcliff Rushmore...Heath...Heath Rushmore... hmm."

"I was named after my grandfather."

I snapped my finger. "So, that's why you go by Rush..."

He feigned surprise. "Wow...you're really smart."

"Shut up." I laughed then said, "Thank you for telling me."

He flashed a hesitant smile. "You didn't give me much of a choice, brat."

CHAPTER 8

Rush

"Heathcliff. It's good to see you, son." My father patted my back, interrupting the conversation I was in the middle of with Gerald Horvath, my grandfather's attorney and always the only friendly face in the room toward me.

"Edward." I nodded.

My father and brother hated my existence, but appearances were important to them. Disdain hid under a masked smile when anyone was around. Especially when that anyone had voting power, as Gerald did.

Grandfather's attorney had just given me the dirty details of the purpose of today's meeting. Vanderhaus owned commercial real estate all over Manhattan, and today's vote was to approve a large property sale without disclosing certain things to the buyer. The board was at odds. My brother, Elliott, and father held forty-nine percent of the company's voting power and were always a united front. I held twenty-five percent, something I'm sure Grandfather had decided on strategically. Individually, my brother and father each held twenty-four-and-a-half percent, so my vote outweighed theirs. But united, they could bulldoze their way through many votes since they only needed to snag one percent to have a majority. Apparently, the vote today was David vs. Goliath, and they hadn't been able to secure anyone's commitment to vote with them yet.

"Your brother and I would love to catch up, if I could steal you away from Gerald for a few minutes."

Gerald knew the blood between the three of us ran thin, but bowed out graciously as always. "Sure. No problem. I see a cheese danish calling my name over there before we start anyway."

Once Gerald was out of earshot, my loving father's mask slipped down just as Elliott joined us. "How much will it take for you to vote with us?"

My father had always assumed me and my mother were all about money. It was incomprehensible to him that someone without any would put their morals and self-respect ahead of making a quick buck.

I sipped a bottled water. "Let me get this straight. You bought a flailing nursing home that the community very much needed." I pointed to my brother. "I'm guessing you're the one who negotiated the purchase by promising the seller that you had every intention of keeping the facility open, but somehow that promise didn't make its way into the contract. Then you demolished the place, along with a few other houses you bought surrounding it. All to make room for an eight-story mall that you could fill with a bunch of overpriced chain stores."

My brother looked me up and down. He must've sucked on a lemon that left his face like that right before he walked over to our lovely chat. "I'll tell you what…" he said, "…you swing your vote our way, and I'll make sure we rent space to a decent, moderately priced, men's suit chain and see to it that you get a twenty-five percent discount."

I smiled and continued, not bothering to trade personal jabs with my arrogant half-brother. "I wasn't quite finished with my story. Then you find out that the soil underneath the building you just tore down is contaminated with lead and a whole list of other toxins. That it will cost you upwards of a million bucks to clean it up, not to mention building delays and dealing with the DEP. Now that the mall is out of the question, you want to sell the property to *another* nursing home company that is interested in building a new facility on the site, and you have no plans to disclose what you've found to the buyer."

"Don't be naïve," my father scolded. "This is the business world we're in. Not some tattoo parlor where you decide not to mar the skin on a drunken girl's ass because she isn't in the right frame of mind to have that rose she's always wanted tattooed on her left cheek. It's caveat emptor—*buyer beware*—we have no legal obligation to coddle a buyer."

"No *legal* obligation. What about an ethical one?"

"You're being ridiculous. Do you know how much money we all stand to lose if we are forced to keep this land and go through with this cleanup?"

"It was the company's mistake in buying the land without testing the soil. It's the company that should pay for it. From what I heard, the nursing home that sold you the property had an environmental study done before they built the place sixty years ago. They'd have no way of knowing what seeped into the soil from the surrounding gas stations over the years. And if you would've kept the property a nursing home—like you told the community you'd planned to—the issue wouldn't have reared its ugly head either."

My brother buttoned his jacket and looked at our father. "I told you it was a waste of time to try to make him understand business. You can take the tattooed boy out of the hood, but you'll never take the hood out of the boy." He turned to me. "With this type of loss, and the way I'm sure you'll run the other businesses Grandfather left you into the ground, you'll be back to tattooing criminals in no time."

I winked at my brother. "Not the drunk ones. Remember, I'm the upstanding brother who believes in not tattooing roses on their asses."

Luckily for me, the secretary called the board meeting to order. For the next two hours we all sat around listening to my father and brother bullshit everyone. I had to hand it to them. They spun such a good tale, for a minute, I almost believed that voting with them to endorse the sale without disclosing the property contamination was in the best interest of the community.

We broke for a break before the formal vote, and I went outside to have a cigarette. Oddly, it was easier to breathe with nicotine-laced, thick smoke filling my lungs than it was in that fancy boardroom.

On the way back to the meeting, I found my brother down a quiet hall with a woman. I almost didn't notice it was him, seeing as his entire face was buried in the woman's neck—a woman who wasn't his wife. *Such a piece of shit.*

He strolled into the meeting at the last minute chatting with a board member and wearing his usual smug smile. I'd seen the board member a few times. I remembered she was the heir to some fortune her dead husband had left and had a British accent—Maribel something was her name. They both took their seats, diagonally across from each other, and the meeting resumed. Not having gotten a good look at the woman from the hall, I really hoped it wasn't her, and he wasn't screwing a board member.

"Alright, let's get this over with," my father said. "This is a public vote. The secretary here has everyone's voting power on his laptop, so all we need to do is hear a yay or a nay on the sale. He'll tally up the results when we're done."

The secretary then proceeded to call off names and people voted.

"No."

"No."

"No."

"No."

After the fourth member voted no, I looked over at my brother. He didn't look at all concerned. When it was my turn, my father shot me a look of disgust for voting my conscience.

Every member voted no, until we got to the one remaining vote, aside from my father and brother—the woman who walked in with my brother. She looked over at him before casting her vote. *Fuck*. Her eyes hooded and, upon closer look, her swollen lips confirmed she was the woman from the hall.

"Maribel Stewart? Your vote?"

"Yes."

Fuck.

All they needed was one person to vote with them.

I stayed in my seat until everyone but my brother and father cleared out of the room. My brother's face was so self-righteous, I had the urge to rearrange it for him.

"I don't know how you sleep at night," I said.

"I have a ten-thousand-dollar bed fit for a king." Elliot grinned.

I stood. "I'd rather sleep on the floor and have a clear conscience."

He fixed his tie and looked up at me. "Fitting, the floor is where you belong."

———

All worked up after the encounter with my dysfunctional family, I texted Gia to see where she was at.

Rush: Where are you?

She responded a few seconds later.

Gia: At Ellen's Stardust Diner on Broadway. Having some lunch. They have the best French toast.

Rush: I'm heading over there.

Since I'd parked my car in a garage for the day, I hopped a cab to the restaurant. The meeting with my father and Elliot was still running through my mind, and I needed to calm the fuck down.

I needed to see Gia.

I knew she'd make me feel better, even though it was frustrating to admit that to myself. Having to curb the urge to smoke in the cab, I rolled down the window and let the cool air hit my face.

I thought about Gia's conning me into telling her my name. That little witch knew my weakness. She knew my jealousy knew no bounds, and she knew exactly how to manipulate that. That was a dangerous talent.

But damn, it worked.

I couldn't help but laugh to myself.

She got me.

Well played, Gia. Well played.

The cabbie was looking at me through the rearview mirror. "Something funny?" he asked in a Jamaican accent.

Busted.

"Nah. Just thinking about a woman who makes me a little crazy."

Nodded in understanding, he said, "Yeah, mon. Don't they all."

He dropped me off, and I entered the diner, which was retro-themed with vinyl red booths and neon lights. One of the servers, dressed in a poodle skirt from the fifties, was standing on top of one of the booths singing. She was probably a wannabe Broadway actress.

It didn't surprise me one bit that Gia had chosen this place. It was eccentric, just like her. What did surprise me was to find her sitting in a booth across from an NYPD officer. Before I could draw the conclusion that she was getting herself in trouble for doing something stupid, I noticed she seemed to be smiling and laughing.

A cop? What the hell?

My fists tightened. A rush of adrenaline hit me until I got closer and realized who it was from the resemblance alone. She *had* said she was planning to meet her father.

Shit.

Her father.

I felt like a dumbass now. With everything that happened back at Vanderhaus, I became distracted and had totally forgotten she was meeting him. I definitely wouldn't have come here if I'd remembered she was with her dad.

It was too late to turn back. She spotted me. So did he.

You could have told me, Gia!

She was smiling from ear to ear and waved me over to their booth. Gia seemed completely comfortable with this situation, which was the opposite of how I was feeling right now.

"Hey!" she said.

Placing my hands in the pockets of my jeans, I nodded once. "Hi."

"This must be Rush," her father said.

She'd told him about me?

"Yes, Dad. This is Rush." She turned to me. "Rush, this is my dad, Tony Mirabelli."

Her father looked like he was in good shape for someone I'd put in his early fifties. They both had the same blue eyes that contrasted their dark hair and olive skin.

I took one hand out of my pocket and extended it. "Nice to meet you, sir."

His handshake was firm while his eyes fell to the tattoos on my arm. He nudged his head toward the table. "Sit. Join us."

I looked over at Gia. "I'm thinking maybe I should come back when you're done with your dad. I don't want to interrupt. I have a few errands I could run."

Tony answered for her, "Nonsense. Take a seat." His tone was not exactly casual. It was more demanding, like *sit the fuck down, motherfucker*.

I no longer felt that I could get out of this situation, so I conceded and planted myself next to Gia. There was a huge plate of half-eaten French toast in front of her. Her father's plate was clean.

A waitress came by and placed a menu in front of me. "Can I get you anything?"

I hadn't eaten all day but didn't feel like making myself too comfortable here, so I said, "Just coffee. Black."

My eyes landed on his. Tony was staring at me intently. For some reason, the theme to *The Sopranos* started playing in my head. Probably the name Tony triggered it. The opening sequence where Tony Soprano is driving over the bridge to Jersey flashed through my mind. That was exactly where I wanted to be—driving over a bridge to Jersey and not staring this man in the face right now.

There weren't many things that made me nervous. But sitting across from a man who's looking at you like he knows you want to spread his daughter's legs apart and eat her out, is definitely one of them. Especially, when the dude is packing a pistol.

He folded his hands together and tilted his head to the side. His expression suddenly turned serious. In fact, he looked pissed. "My daughter tells me you punched her in the eye."

My heart started to pound faster. A long moment of silence passed as I just sat there speechless.

She what?

What in the ever-living fuck?

Then...Gia snorted. Tony looked at her, and they both busted out into laughter.

Am I being punked?

"I'm just kidding, son." He wiped his eyes. "It was a joke."

They were both assholes. My pulse finally calmed down.

Can't believe I fell for that.

"He knows the truth about what happened," she said.

I looked him dead in the face. "If I had been there to monitor things, she wouldn't have gotten that black eye. I'm sorry she got hurt."

He simply nodded.

"We were just talking about you before you walked in," Gia said.

"Must have been why my ears were ringing."

Tony turned to me. "I hear you gave Gia a job and that you make sure she's safe in getting home at night.

I never really loved the idea of her moving out there all alone and so far away from me when I have no choice but to be here for work. But you know Gia. She has a mind of her own, couldn't be stopped. So, I really appreciate any help I can get in looking out for her."

I felt like a fraud. My thoughts when it came to Gia were far from "safe."

Nevertheless, I took credit. "No problem. It's my pleasure."

He brushed a piece of food off his navy uniform. "I raised my daughter to be smart and independent. But there's only so much she can do to protect herself. I worry about her, particularly because she can be hotheaded like her dad. She can be minding her own business one minute and breaking up a bar fight the next."

"Well, I can definitely agree with you on that one." I chuckled. "Gia is definitely...spirited."

Gia winked at me. She seemed to be enjoying this interaction, whereas I was watching the clock, rearing to leave.

The waitress set a glass of water and a steaming mug of coffee in front of me. I took a sip of the hot liquid.

Tony was just watching me and then caught me off guard when he said, "So...that being said...in all seriousness, what exactly *are* your intentions when it comes to my daughter?"

I nearly spit out my coffee.

A long moment of silence passed before they once again turned to each other and burst into laughter. These two were in cahoots—a couple of pranksters.

VI KEELAND & PENELOPE WARD

Tony cackled and pointed. "I loved the look on your face."

"Don't worry," Gia said as she placed her hand on my forearm. "He knows you're not interested in me and that you're harmless, despite how dangerous you might look." Leaning her shoulder against mine, she said, "Right, Rush? He has *nothing* to worry about?" She batted her eyelashes at me.

I swallowed. "That's right."

The better to eat you with, my dear,
Said the big bad wolf.

She addressed her father, "Rush says because he's my boss, we can't date."

He took a sip of water then said, "Well, that's smart, I suppose. Never hurts to keep things professional."

I glared at Gia. "I completely agree."

"Although, you're probably kidding yourself," Tony said. "I see the way you look at my daughter, and I'm not sure I like it, to be honest."

My eyes narrowed.

Shit.

He must have sensed the worry on my face when he said, "Man, you're gullible."

He was fucking with me again. Gia and her dad were once again laughing at me. Two peas in a pod.

"You want to know the truth, son?"

I let out a long breath. "Sure..."

"I did my best to lead by example as far as my daughter is concerned, show her what a good, decent, hardworking man is like. I trust her judgment. So, if Gia feels that someone is worthy of her time and trust, then that's enough for me, whether it's a friend or more. Who she associates with...well, it's not my decision to make anymore."

I nodded once. "Alright..."

"Plus, I ran a full background check on you a little while ago as soon as she told me about you. Came up clear." He grinned. "Heathcliff Rushmore. Interesting name."

Thanks a fucking lot, Gia.

Gritting my teeth, I said, "It's a family name."

"Speaking of family...your father is Edward Vanderhaus..."

Hearing him mention that name made my skin crawl.

"I'm quite aware of that, yes. He's my biological father, but he didn't raise me."

"I was on patrol once for a private event in the City that Vanderhaus booked. He's kind of a dick. No offense."

"None taken. And believe me, I'm quite aware of that." I sighed. "What did he do?"

"It wasn't so much what he did...just the way he spoke to people, you know? Just my observation."

"Yup. I know exactly what you mean."

"Gia was telling me everything—about your inheritance. You don't have to go into it. Very interesting story, though, to say the least."

I turned to her. "Did you talk about anything *other* than me today, Gia?"

She shrugged. "Sorry. But I tell my dad everything."

"I can see that." I offered a slight smile so she didn't actually think I was mad at her. I could've cared less what her father knew. I had nothing to hide.

The waitress came by to refill my coffee and warmed Tony's, too.

He gulped some of it down then said, "Sounds like you've done the best you can with all that you've been given, son—the good and the bad."

"At heart, I'm still a blue-collar guy from Long Island. I saw how hard my mother struggled. I never expected things to be handed to me. I still work hard and don't take anything for granted."

"Well, this poor boy from Queens finds that admirable."

Gia interrupted, "He's fixing my car for me, too, Dad."

"You know your way around cars?"

"Yeah. I used to work in an auto repair shop."

Tony seemed impressed. "No kidding..."

"He also used to be a tattoo artist," Gia said. "I asked him if he could ink me, but he refuses."

"Sounds like he knows you can be a little impulsive. Good call, Rush."

I almost wished Gia's dad were more of a dick. It would give me another good reason to stay away from her. He'd raised her all on his own and seemed to have done a hell of a job. I hated to say it, but Tony was cool as shit, the kind of man I wished I had for a father.

He looked down at his watch. "Well, as much as I'd love to stay with you, sweetheart, work beckons. I've got to get back to the precinct."

Gia pouted. "Alright, Daddy. I'm glad we got to see each other." She stood up and gave him a hug.

He held out his hand. "Rush...it was a pleasure. Stay out of trouble." He gave me a look and for some reason that one seemed serious.

Stay out of trouble.

Translation: Stay out of Gia.

CHAPTER 9

Gia

Rush had asked if I was in a hurry to return to the Hamptons. Since it was my night off, I told him there was no reason I had to get back by a certain time.

After we left Ellen's, he said he wanted to get something to eat, which was odd because we'd just spent the last hour at a diner.

Apparently, it wasn't that he hadn't wanted to eat at the restaurant but that he had his heart set on Gray's Papaya hot dogs. We left Gray's with a bag full of wieners.

Rush walked and ate at the same time. "Whenever I come to the City, I just have to have one," he said, biting into the hotdog, which was loaded with chili and cheese.

"One? You ordered ten!"

"They're not all for me," Rush said with his mouth full.

"Who are they for?"

"Some friends. You'll meet them in a bit."

Hmm. I was going to meet his friends?

He held up his hotdog. "Wanna bite?"

"I'm full, thanks."

The sun was coming down over the City. It was a gorgeous evening.

About fifteen minutes later, we stopped at an alleyway, and I immediately figured out who his friends were. Rush had taken the bag of hotdogs to a few homeless men who were gathered in the alley with their belongings stuffed into black trash bags.

"Hey, guys."

One of them seemed to recognize him. "Hey, Rush, man. How's it goin'?"

"What's good?" Rush asked, handing the entire bag over to him.

"Nothing...you know...the usual."

"Thought you might be hungry."

"Starving. Thank you," the man said. "Who's your pretty friend?"

"This is Gia."

I waved. "Hello."

Rush then reached into his wallet and handed the guy a one-hundred-dollar bill. "Promise me, you won't spend it on booze."

"You got it. I promise."

Rush pointed his two fingers to his eyes and then back at the man. "I'm watching you, Tommy. Take care of yourself, okay?"

As we walked away, I whispered, "That was really nice of you."

He waited until we were no longer within earshot of the men to say, "A long time ago, I decided that a good way to wash away the negativity I feel toward my family's greed is to counter it with something charitable. I told myself every time I come to the City for an obligatory business meeting, that I'd help someone in some way before I leave. Makes me feel good."

"That's really commendable."

"Nah. I have the means. I don't even feel a dent. It would only be commendable if it were a sacrifice. Not like I'm giving anyone the shirt off my back."

"I don't agree. It's the thought that counts, no matter how much money you have. You're a good guy, Rush. And you would give anyone the shirt off your back if they needed it. I've only known you for a short time, but I have no doubt about that."

His ears seemed to turn red. I was learning that Rush wasn't comfortable taking compliments.

He stopped for a moment. "Anywhere you want to go before we head back?"

Starting to feel tired, I said, "I think I'd just like to go home. I have to write tonight."

We started walking again when he asked, "How's it coming anyway? The book?"

I sighed. "It's not really...coming."

His mouth twitched and he looked tense.

"What's up?" I asked.

"You said *coming*. I lost my train of thought for a second."

"Forgot I have to be careful with my words around you." I winked.

"Seriously, though," he said. "Why do you think you're having so much trouble focusing?"

"I just can't stop the self-doubt. I second-guess every word and erase what I wrote half of the time. It's awful."

Rush scratched his chin. "Why don't you try to write as if no one is going to read it? Just say fuck it... and stop overthinking it. I bet if you go back and read what you wrote afterward, you'll find it's not even that bad. Having something down on paper is better than nothing at all."

I pondered his advice. "So, pretend that no one will ever see it..."

"Yeah. If you find yourself stopping to think too much...just keep going...push through it. Worry about it later. Write the first thing that comes to mind and trust your instinct. You're probably a way worse judge of yourself than anyone." He nudged me with his shoulder. "Anyway, who cares what people think? Write what *you* like...I bet it will turn out that's what other people will like, too."

Nodding, I considered his advice. "I'll try to adopt that approach." His words repeated it my mind and prompted me to say, "But that's pretty ironic coming from you, don't you think?"

"What part is ironic?"

"'Who cares what people think?' This from the guy who refuses to date an employee for fear of what everyone will think?"

He slowed his pace, looking a bit pissed at me for bringing this up. "It's not about what people think, so much as the principle of the matter. As a business owner, you don't date someone you employ. It's unethical. It's also ripe pickings for a lawsuit and that's a headache I sure as hell don't need."

"But it's okay for you to sleep in my bed?"

That comment seemed to anger him even more. "No, that's not okay. That was a mistake."

The question that had been on the tip of my tongue somehow slipped out against my better judgment. "What if I got another job? Would that change things?"

He seemed to be struggling with how to respond to that. I braced myself because I knew the answer to that question was a game changer. It would prove his true feelings once and for all.

Rush reached into his pocket for a cigarette before lighting up. It had seemed like he was making a conscious effort not to smoke up until I drove him to it just now.

His eyes almost looked pained when he said, "I like hanging out with you. But I'm not right for you, Gia."

"Then the boss thing is just an excuse? It's really not the reason you won't date me."

"It's not the only issue, no. The issue is me...not you."

I rolled my eyes. "It's not you. It's me. What an original line! I should put that in my sucky book."

———

My little interrogation must have angered Rush more than I knew, because he was quiet the rest of the walk to the parking garage.

Once we got to the car and on the road, the silent treatment continued as he proceeded to just smoke the entire time.

I was mad at myself for bringing up the subject of our relationship. He'd made his intentions clear, and I had to accept that. But there was still the fact that I wasn't sure if I fully believed he didn't want more with me. He was clearly attracted to me and protective of me. Was he scared? Or just not interested? It didn't matter. As soon as he'd pulled the old "it's not you, it's me," I was done.

I couldn't stand the quiet anymore, so I was the first to speak.

"You said we were gonna play fortunately-unfortunately on the ride back."

"Yeah, well, I'm not in the mood right now."

Ignoring him, I said, "Okay...I'll start. Fortunately, one of us doesn't stay angry for very long and knows how to break the ice."

He gave me side-eye and surprised me when he started to play along. "Unfortunately, Gia decided to break the ice by reminding me of this stupid game." He shook his head and blew smoke out the window.

"Fortunately, Gia's not sensitive, otherwise you calling her game *stupid* would have upset her."

"Unfortunately, I think Gia *is* sensitive and takes certain things personally when she really shouldn't."

"Fortunately, Gia doesn't have to be told twice, so you don't have to worry about her inquiring about the status of our relationship anymore ever again."

He lit up another cigarette before he said, "Unfortunately, I think that's for the best."

"Fortunately, I now understand that we are, in fact, just friends."

His expression dampened. A few seconds passed before he responded with, "Unfortunately, I have to apologize for my actions that have led you to believe otherwise."

"Fortunately—for you—I forgive you."

"Unfortunately, this means I can't sleep in your bed anymore, either."

I admired his apology, but that didn't stop me from wanting to stick it to him.

"Fortunately, now that you've made your feelings clear, this frees me up to accept the date I've been putting off with Rhys, the roof bartender."

CHAPTER 10

Rush

"**B**ring the kegs up to the rooftop bar," I snapped at the shadow of a man passing by my office. The hall was dark, but I knew exactly who it was. The asshole had been on my radar ever since Gia dropped a bomb in the car on the way home from the City.

"Me?" Rhys took a step back into the doorway of the office. I didn't bother to lift my head from the paperwork I had my nose buried in.

"Who the fuck else would I be talking to? Is there another person in the vicinity?" I still didn't look up.

"Umm. Oak usually carries them upstairs. Those things weigh a hundred-sixty pounds."

Of course, I knew exactly what they weighed, and I was pretty sure that the things outweighed his skinny ass. I looked up, my bloodshot eyes beaded with contempt. "Are you saying you're incapable of performing your job?"

"Uh...no. No. I'll...I'll get them up there." He continued to stand there, staring.

"Are you waiting for something?" I bit out. "Get to work."

VI KEELAND & PENELOPE WARD

"Umm. Sure. Right. Yes, boss." Even though he said that, when he saw me get up and head over to the door, the pansy-ass stayed frozen in place. For a heartbeat, when his eyes grew wide, and I thought he might shit his pants, I almost felt bad for the guy. *Almost.* Though that notion wore off before I slammed the door in the fucker's face.

For the last three days, I'd managed to avoid Gia. I'd been planning a renovation of one of the rental properties I owned out here, and the permits finally came through from the town. While the demolition crew I hired ripped out the dated kitchen and back deck, I spent most of the days meeting subcontractors to get quotes on doing the remodel. Even though I could afford the extra cost of hiring a GC to do that type of shit, I liked to manage my own construction projects. And God knows, I could use the fucking distraction from spending all my time watching over Gia at this place.

My cell phone rang, and the first genuine smile I had in days appeared on my face. I sat back into my chair while I answered. "Well if it isn't the birthday girl. Sleep in? I called you two hours ago."

"I was actually out getting supplies," my mother said. "The phone rang while I was driving, and I don't know how to hook up the hands-free thing. You'll have to do that for me this weekend."

"Alright."

"I bought a new set of acrylics and some extra canvas. I'm hoping the sunset is as beautiful as it was last year out there."

"The weather is supposed to be nice. When are you coming out?"

"This afternoon, if you don't mind. I know I usually come out on Friday, but I need to get back early to help out at the summer cookout they're having at church."

"Of course. Whatever you want. You're welcome anytime. You know that. Let yourself in when you get here, and I'll try to be home early from the restaurant. I'll bring home a nice birthday dinner with me."

"Actually…I was thinking of coming to the restaurant for the sunset tonight to paint, if that won't interrupt your busy time or anything. I won't take up much room, just a chair in the corner of the rooftop bar. I don't even need to bring my easel."

"Bring anything you want. I'll close the fucking place if having other people around distracts you."

"Heathcliff…*your language.*"

I was transported back to being ten again. "Sorry. I'll try to watch my mouth. But can you lay off the Heathcliff around my place of business. No one knows my name is anything other than just Rush. I'm like Madonna…only with a bigger di…. Never mind, just call me Rush at work, please, Ma."

"Okay, sweetheart. I'll see you in a few hours."

———

It was almost five by the time I emerged from my office. I hated to sit behind a desk all day, which was the primary reason it took me the entire afternoon to catch up on all the paperwork I'd been avoiding. The kitchen staff had arrived and were here prepping for the start of the dinner rush when I stopped in.

"I need something that isn't on tonight's menu made, probably for about seven o'clock."

"Sure thing, Rush. Whatta ya need?" Fred, the head chef asked. He'd been my first hire when I took over the place five years ago.

"Salmon Oscar. Just like you used to make at McCormick and Schmick's."

He pointed a pair of tongs in his hand at me and smiled. "You got it. Whatever you're in the mood for."

"It's actually not for me. But I appreciate it. I'll probably just order a burger to eat later."

"Hot date?"

"It's my mom's birthday. She'll be here in a little while."

Fred winked. "I'll make it better than I made it when I worked at McCormick and Schmick's, then."

I figured I'd head upstairs to section off a little area for my mom to paint before she got here. Thursdays were busy, but usually more so after the dinner rush ended. By then, the sunset would be long gone, and she wasn't a late-night person anyway.

Climbing the stairs two at a time with a cushioned indoor chair in my hand, I hit the rooftop and froze. We hadn't opened yet, but my staff was busy setting up tables and stocking the outdoor bar. Everyone bustled around getting ready, except for my bartender. *Rhys.* Instead of working, he had his forearms resting on the bar while he flirted with a woman. And not just any woman. The smiling asshole was standing there flirting with *my girl.*

Fury pumped through my veins as I stood there watching. Rhys said something I couldn't hear, and Gia threw her head back laughing. *Fuck.* She was so beautiful when she smiled.

As if she sensed me watching her, Gia's head turned and our eyes caught. She straightened her spine and jutted her chin out, almost daring me to do something about whatever I'd just walked out to see.

She isn't even on tonight. What the fuck is she doing here?

It took every bit of willpower I had in me to not walk over there and punch the little peckerhead she was talking to in the face. But somehow I managed to control myself. Taking a deep breath, I didn't acknowledge her. Instead, I went about my own business. I pulled a table over to the corner that had the best sunset views, stuck a *reserved* sign on it, and then set up a comfortable chair so my mom would have a place to paint.

When I was done, I yelled over to the bartender who was now enemy number one. "This is reserved for tonight. If anyone sits here or takes that chair, you're fired."

I didn't wait for an answer.

Back downstairs, I put my anger to use, bellowing at my staff to move their asses. They looked at me like I was a ticking time bomb, although with the insane amount of rage I felt in my chest, I wasn't quite sure they were that off base.

Needing to calm down, I stomped toward the bar, poured myself a shot of whiskey, and knocked it back before heading outside for a cigarette. The smoke soothed the fire in my throat when it should have fanned the flame.

I smelled her before I heard her voice. Lost in my head, I hadn't even noticed Gia open or close the door behind me. "Hey. There you are. Is everything okay?"

"Fine," I clipped out and inhaled again deeply until the ember tip of my cigarette turned a bright shade of orange.

"I wasn't trying to stop Rhys from working, if that's what pissed you off. I carried up a few bottles of rum, knowing there is a drink special on the menu with rum in it tonight."

I responded in a more bitter tone than I'd intended. "Why are you here?"

"I'm working tonight. I guess Carla didn't tell you? We switched tonight for Saturday night because she had something to do."

My face was blank. "No. She didn't tell me. Why *the fuck* would anyone tell me anything around here? I only own the damn place."

"You're in a mood. Do you want to talk about it?"

"No, Gia. *I don't want to talk about it.* I just want all of my staff to go about their business and keep *the hell* out of mine. Is that so fucking hard to do?"

She blinked a few times, her face looked like I'd just physically slapped her. "No. That's not so hard to do, *boss*. Forgive me if I overstepped and gave a shit because you looked like you might be upset." She turned to leave, stopping as she opened the door. "It won't happen again."

My mom showed up at six o'clock. I was talking to a DJ who stopped by to discuss the upcoming Fourth of July party I'd hired him for, when I saw her out of the corner of my eye. She smiled spotting me, and it was the first time I felt my shoulders loosen enough to breathe comfortably today.

"Hey, Ma." I swamped her in a big hug. My mom was a tiny little thing. She liked to tease that I'd almost killed her giving birth to my ten-pound pudgy ass. My size was the one thing that I'd clearly gotten from my father that I didn't hate.

"Happy fifty-second birthday."

She smiled. "Shhh. I'm thirty-eight this year."

In all honestly, no one would blink twice if she said she was thirty-eight. Melody Rushmore kept herself in great shape with daily yoga and some sort of transcendental meditation that she always tried to get me to try out. Looking at her, people would never know that she had a tough life. The youngest of four children raised in rural Canada by an abusive father and alcoholic mother, she moved to New York City at only eighteen. She met my asshole father at twenty-two and fell for his bullshit. Eighteen months later, when she was two months pregnant with me, his true colors came out when he demanded she get an abortion. Before that, she'd had no idea that he was married. Definitely no clue that his wife had just given birth to a son of their own just six months earlier. Since dear old dad wasn't about to own up to his responsibilities without a paternity test, Mom had to stop working at her dream job at the art gallery and find a job the provided insurance. She'd given up a lot for me, even before I was born.

"Is your easel in the car?"

"Yes. But I don't need to use it. I can just put a canvas on my lap."

"Don't be ridiculous. Let me get you something to drink, and then I'll go grab your stuff from the car."

I walked Mom to the bar, my eyes trained on the adjoining dining room where some fuckwad in a cheap suit was checking out Gia's ass while she walked him to a table. *The fucking universe is out to test my patience tonight.*

Distracted, I poured Mom a glass of wine that almost overflowed. "Let me have your keys. I'll be right back."

Cheap Suit was still molesting Gia with his eyes. On my way to Mom's car, I walked over to the table he still hadn't sat his ass down at. "Everything okay here?" My face did not look like it gave a flying fuck if it was.

Gia's brows furrowed. "Fine. Did you need something?"

I glared at Cheap Suit. "Just for your customers to take their seat so you can get back to work."

Gia glared back on his behalf. "Thank you. If we need any assistance, we'll let you know."

I stormed off to the car. At the door, Oak shot me a knowing grin that said he'd just watched the interaction I had with my employee. I pointed a finger at him. "Don't say a fucking word." Then crashed the front door to the restaurant open.

The gravel beneath my feet crunched like it was as pissed off as I was while I made my way through the parking lot to find Mom's car. Grabbing her paints, canvas, easel, and brushes, I slammed the trunk to her Kia and leaned against the car with my eyes shut.

The sound of gravel-chomping footsteps interrupted my attempt at calming myself. Gia was headed right toward me again and looked as pissed as I felt. I looked up at the sky and grumbled, "Not again."

Her tiny hands flew to her hips. "This is bullshit."

"You walking out of the restaurant when you should be inside working? I couldn't fucking agree more."

She squinted at me. "You know what I'm talking about."

I pushed off the car and took a step forward. "I'm not in the mood for your psycho-analysis bullshit, Gia. Go back inside and get to work."

"I thought you were different than all the other Hamptonite jerk guys. But the truth is, you just wear different armor on the outside. On the inside you're the same self-absorbed, narcissistic bastard they all are."

"*I'm* self-absorbed? Because I want you to do your job and not stick your tits in the face of my staff and customers."

If I'd thought she was pissed off before, her face contorted to a whole new level of angry. Her lips twisted into a scowl, her forehead pinched, and the color in her face turned a lovely shade of crimson. At that moment, it became clear that I was losing my fucking mind, because while I'd been pissed off and wanting to lash out at the world since I'd first saw that skinny bartender pass my office earlier today, suddenly Gia's seething changed my mood.

I bet angry fucking her would be great.

She stood in front of me practically foaming at the mouth, and all I saw was me, holding a fistful of her hair, yanking hard as I plowed into her from behind, smacking her ass over and over.

Fuck.

"You're an egomaniac. You don't want me, but you don't want me to show anyone else any attention, either."

I stared at her, her words blurring as more visions became clear: Wrists tied to my headboard while she writhed under my tongue. I'd suck her pussy until she was on edge, just about to let go, then I'd lift her legs up into the air and onto my shoulders. Spreading her wetness from clit to crack, I'd lube up her tight little virgin ass. And then finger fuck the shit out of it until she was begging all over again.

"Blah. Blah Blah." At least that's what I heard. Gia's voice was going again, but I couldn't make out a damn word if I tried.

"Are you even listening to me?" she barked.

Not a fucking word. But turn around, bend over the hood of Mom's car, and I'll hear every scream I can wring out of you.

God, I really hoped her ass had never been touched. *Would she punch me if I asked right now? Do I give a flying fuck if she does?*

"What the hell is wrong with you?" she continued to stare at me like I had two heads.

A dark smirk tugged at the corners of my mouth. "Can I ask you a personal question?"

"*What?*" Her patience ran thin.

My eyes dropped to the heavy heave of her chest, her nipples angrily protruding. God, she was sexy as fuck pissed off. Asking the status of her asshole would certainly elevate that...

I took a step forward and leaned down so our faces were aligned. She stood her ground with a swallow. "Anyone ever enter through your back door, Gia?"

Her pissed-off face morphed into confusion. "What? I came out the front door. Didn't you just see me walk out?"

"I was talking about your *ass*, Gia."

It took a minute for her to figure out what the hell I meant. But I knew the minute she did. A storm swept the calm sea blue of her eyes into dark churning waters. She took a step back, and I thought she was turning to walk away. That is, until I realized she was only winding up to smack me straight across the face.

CHAPTER 11

Gia

He had some balls.

Giant ones. The kind that I wouldn't miss if my foot happened to attempt a swift kick. Which I definitely hadn't ruled out.

I seated an older couple at a table and watched from a distance as the asshole flirted with a woman at the bar. He'd been standing there since he walked back inside with my handprint etched into his face. Obviously the sting in my heart hurt more than what my hand had done to him, since he was already laughing and flirting, enjoying himself while I continued to stew.

The woman got up, and Rush's hand went to her back. There was a familiarity in his touch and in their interaction. She was probably one of his summer fucks. He guided her to the stairs that led up to the roof while I gaped from a distance.

She was definitely older than him. I'd guess late thirties or even early forties. Unlike the other woman I'd seen hanging around the bar drooling over him, this one wasn't dressed like a whore. She had on a pair of jeans, rolled at the ankle, and a baggy, oversized T-shirt that hung almost to her knees. A pair of flip-flops with a big daisy flower on each donned her feet, rather than the usual stilettos his casual fucks seemed to like to wear.

Are you shitting me?

He had the audacity to speak to me the way he had outside, and now he just casually moved on to some May-December hookup right under my nose?

No.

Just no.

Weaving through patrons, I made my way to the stairwell. Running up to the rooftop, I could feel my pulse racing.

I stopped upon the sight of Rush pulling out a chair for his lady friend before sitting down across from her. They looked very comfortable together, and he was— dare I say—smiling like a fool.

My blood was boiling. I watched intently as he walked over to the bar and ordered her a glass of wine, bringing it back to the table.

My breathing was ragged as I continued to stand in the entrance observing them from afar—until I lost it.

Storming over to the table, I huffed, "Are you kidding me right now?"

Rush stood up suddenly and held out his hands in an apparent attempt to stop my outburst. "Gia...thi—"

"No!" I refused to back down. "I'm sorry. I'm *not* gonna shut up."

"Gia!" he yelled louder.

The bar was crowded, and no one seemed to be paying attention to this confrontation aside from Rush's date whose eyes were fixed on me.

Ignoring his plea, I got in his face. "What kind of a game are you playing? One second you're outside asking me if I've ever been fucked in the ass and the next second, you're upstairs wining and dining some woman? What's wrong with you?"

His date cringed.

Rush gritted his teeth. "Stop!"

"No, I wo—"

He lifted me off my feet. Before I knew it, I was being literally carried out of the bar area.

Kicking my legs, I screamed, "What do you think you're doing?"

He didn't answer me as he continued on to the hallway by the stairwell and put me down before backing me up against a wall.

His eyes were searing into mine, but he said nothing as customers brushed by us to enter the rooftop area.

Still bleeding jealousy, I panted. "Who was that woman?"

He stared at me for several seconds before he finally spat out, "That's not a *woman*. That's my mother!"

A rush of blood suddenly coursed through my veins.

No.

This couldn't be happening.

"Your..." I cleared my throat. "You're lying. That's not...she's...I just...oh...oh, no...no." I held onto my head with both hands. "I didn't just say that...in front of your mother?"

"Yes." He nodded. "Yes, you fucking did."

I was panicked. "Oh God. Rush, I'm so sorry. I didn't know."

Rush looked like he was ready to blow.

"Get back to work," he demanded. "And stay the fuck off the rooftop."

"Rush..." I pleaded.

Seething, he started to walk away, leaving me in the hallway. He turned around, and when he saw I hadn't moved, he barked louder, "Go!"

———

I didn't know how long I'd been staring into space before Oak interrupted, "You okay, Gia? You look pale."

It was just about closing time. Rush hadn't come downstairs once since I'd made an ass of myself—no pun intended—in front of his mom. Even though I'd wanted to just go home, somehow, I'd managed to muddle through the rest of my shift.

Turning to him, I felt like crying. "I screwed up, Oak...in a really big way."

Oak pulled up a chair next to where I was standing. "Want to tell me what happened?"

"I really don't want to say."

"Let me guess. This has something to do with the boss?"

Rolling my eyes, I said, "How ever did you know?"

"Wild guess." He sighed. "I don't even know what happened, but I suspect it involved Rush blowing his top over something?"

"Oh, he blew his top, alright."

Oak looked almost entertained by my dilemma.

He began to tell me a story. "So...my daughter, Jazzy...she's in fifth grade, right? I got called to the school the other day because there's this boy who's been bothering her...teasing her, pulling her hair...stuff like that."

"Yeah?"

"The boy's mother showed up at this meeting, too. You know what she told me? She said all this kid talks about at home is Jazzy. He seems to have a crush on her, but he has a funny way of showing it."

I joked, "What ever are you getting at, Oak?"

He raised his brow. "I think you can draw your own conclusions there."

Feeling flush, I said, "Well, tonight had nothing to do with Rush's feelings or lack of feelings toward me. Tonight was one-hundred percent my fault." Blowing out a breath, I decided to tell him what happened. "I assumed that Rush's mother was his date earlier, confronted him in anger upstairs, and said something *really* bad in front of her. I can't ever take it back, and I'm pretty sure he wants to kill me now."

"Ouch. Okay. Wow. Well...first of all, I suspect the boss wants to do a lot of things when it comes to you, Gia, but murder isn't one of them." He laughed. "Anyway, how bad could it really be? What did you say that was so awful?"

I shook my head. "I can't even repeat it. Ironically, I was paraphrasing something *he* said to *me* privately. I want to throw up."

"Well, let's back up for a second. The good news is... Melody is very down to Earth. She probably laughed it off. She doesn't strike me as a prude. I'm sure Rush has explained the situation to her by now."

"What situation? That he has a nutjob working for him who yells out sexually explicit things in the middle of a crowded bar...in front of his *mother*?"

"*Sexually* explicit? Dang. Sucks to be you."

"Yeah. *Dang*. It does."

"I'm kidding." He laughed.

Sighing, I said, "Seriously, I don't even know what I would say to her if she were standing in front of me."

His eyes gestured to behind my shoulders. "Well... now's your chance to find out."

What?

I slowly turned to find Rush's mother standing there.

My heart dropped. "Oh...hello, Mrs....*Ms*. Rushmore."

"Please call me Melody, Gia."

She knew my name. Then again, Rush had yelled it out in a failed attempt to stop me from making a fool of myself.

God, she was really pretty. Her shoulder-length, light brown hair was colored ombre, blonder at the ends. Her blue eyes were glowing. She sort of reminded me of a young Goldie Hawn. And she was short—like me. It was weird to think that this little woman pushed a big guy like Rush out of her.

"Hello." I smiled awkwardly.

Oak seemed amused. "Good to see you, Miss Melody. Looking beautiful tonight, as always."

She waved. "Hi, Oak."

He stood up like he was rearing to leave. That was not good, because he was the only buffer I had.

Please don't go.

Oak then slipped away, leaving me alone with Rush's mom.

She was the first to speak after a brief moment of silence. "My son forbade me from coming to introduce myself to you, but unfortunately for him, he's not the boss of me."

Her smile definitely calmed me down.

"I'm really glad you came to find me. I didn't have the guts to do the same because I feel awful, like *really* mortified about what I said to him upstairs in front of you. That was so disrespectful and not language I typically use. I had no idea you were his mother. Quite honestly...you look way too young. I assumed you were his date and I was...jealous."

"Well, flattery will get you everywhere." She grinned. "I understand you were upset. No harm done. We've all said and done things in the heat of the moment."

She smiled again and I smiled back.

"Anyway, I can't tell you enough how much I regret my words. I'm sorry for making a scene."

"I appreciate your apology, but it's really okay."

I looked around. "Where's Rush?"

"He got caught up in some business...something about a liquor delivery that was supposed to have been made before tomorrow, but it never showed up. I took advantage...came and found you. Hope you don't mind."

"No, not at all."

"Am I interrupting you at work?" she asked.

"No, my shift just ended, actually. It's closing time."

"My son explained everything to me, that you didn't know who I was and that he actually provoked your outburst earlier. I suppose I should be apologizing for *his* behavior toward *you*."

It surprised me that Rush took any of the blame and that he had been so open with his mother. Still, it was me who made the scene out there. I made the decision to use that language in front of her. There was no way I was going to let this all fall on him.

"I take full responsibility for what I said. It's not like me to use such language so freely, especially in a public place, and especially at my job. Sometimes things get heated between him and me. Your son...well...he's driving me a little crazy."

Melody nodded in understanding. "I don't envy you there. He's not an easy one to navigate, my Heathcliff." She closed her eyes briefly then covered her mouth in laughter. "I mean, *Rush*. Sorry. Old habit. He'd kill me if he knew I just let that slip."

"It's okay...I know Heathcliff is his real name."

She looked shocked. "He told you?"

"I got it out of him, yeah."

"Good for you."

After a few seconds of awkward silence, I said, "So... I'm out of luck, huh?"

She bobbed her head to the side. "How do you mean?"

"In the romance department? Your son's a lost cause?"

"I didn't say that. When I say he's not an easy one...I just mean he's not easy to read. It's not always *easy* to get him to open up. My son has a big heart. But that's not something that people can figure out very easily about him. He's complicated, and it just takes a while to peel back his layers."

"I'm definitely learning that."

"Rush has learned a lot of tough lessons. He's been hurt by people who are supposed to love him. Even though he acts like he doesn't care about that, it's definitely had an effect on the way he lives his life, with his guard constantly up."

I frowned. "I know all about his dad, yeah."

She was examining my face. "He's fond of you."

My heart sped up. "He said that?"

"No, not in so many words. But he seemed very concerned that I would think negatively of you. It's not like him to talk to me at all about women he's friendly with. His personal life is just something he's always kept to himself. But he told me a little about you over dinner...told me you're a writer."

"He did?"

"Yes."

That reminded me...

"By the way..." I said. "I want to thank you, actually. Rush once told me that when you get stuck in your art process, that you sometimes go to see a movie to break out of your funk. I actually tried that once and it worked. After that, I had one of the best writing days I'd had in a long time."

"Oh, that's wonderful. Yes, that's one of my strategies for sure. I'm glad it worked for you, too."

"Do you come visit him here at The Heights often? I haven't seen you here before...obviously."

"I drive out here once every month or two." Melody was delicate and soft-spoken, not at all like her son. "I wanted to capture the sunset over the ocean on canvas tonight."

"You painted here tonight?"

"Yes. Rush set up my easel upstairs on the roof earlier."

"That's so neat. Can I see what you made?"

She looked thrilled that I'd asked. "Sure."

I looked around nervously for Rush as I followed her up to the roof. She led me to a canvas painting that was leaning up against the wall in the corner.

She held it up to show me. "It's not exactly perfect, but I'm happy with how it came out."

With blends of orange, purple and yellow, she had beautifully captured the stunning colors of the evening sunset over the beach. Smudges of paint accurately portrayed the clouds in the sky. I couldn't begin to fathom how she'd made the ocean so realistic with a mix of green, blue, and white tones. It somehow looked like the water was moving across the canvas, coming into shore. My favorite part of the whole painting was a single and elaborately detailed seashell with brown and white lines drawn throughout. It was just laid out on the sand, which she'd meticulously painted in beige hues. Even though the shell was small, it seemed to be the focus to which all else served as the backdrop.

"This is so beautiful. I am seriously in awe that you have the ability to sit down and casually paint something so amazing on a whim. How long did it take you?"

She placed the painting on the ground, leaning it against the table leg. "About an hour-and-a-half. But you know, it's not always that easy for me. Maybe you go through this with your writing, but some days you're just *on*, right? You can feel the creativity oozing from your veins, and you just need to drop everything and take advantage while it's there. That's why I needed to come to the beach tonight." Her eyes were filled with passion as she spoke about her art.

This woman is amazing.

"I *so* get what you're saying, Melody," I said. "I used to feel like that from time to time when I first got the idea for this book I'm writing. The first three chapters just poured out of me, very organically like that. And then once I started to apply pressure on myself after I landed the publishing deal, nothing has been happening."

"Rush said that you write in the romance genre?"

Once again, I was surprised he'd gone into that much detail with her.

"Yes. Contemporary. Well, if I can ever get going again, yeah."

"Nothing like pressure to hinder creativity. I can relate. A few of my pieces have been commissioned in the past. There's definitely a difference between creating something out of your own free will versus obligation."

"Exactly."

"You'll find your way—your inspiration, Gia. It will happen."

Can I keep her?

"Thank you. I hope so."

We stood there just staring at each other momentarily. If I didn't know better, I'd think she really liked me, too. I wasn't ready to let her go. Melody Rushmore fascinated me.

The words just fell out of me. "I would love to see more of your paintings sometime." I hoped I wasn't being too forward as I anticipated her response.

"Well, you're welcome down to my house whenever you like. I have a studio there filled with art."

"Honestly? I would really love that."

Rush came up behind me. "What's this, now?"

He reeked of smoke. My pulse raced. I couldn't gauge his reaction to my hanging out with his mom. But I played it cool.

"You're taking me to see your mom's studio. I want to see her paintings—all of them."

His brow lifted as if to challenge that. "Is that right?"

I crossed my arms. "Yup."

"If I'd known you two were conferring, I would've hurried my ass up," he said.

His mother was grinning at him. "Gia and I have a lot in common."

"Yeah, you're both pains in my ass," he teased, winking at Melody.

She must have been used to his sarcasm because she didn't react to that statement. I was relieved that he didn't seem too mad anymore.

"Are you heading back home tonight?" I asked her.

"No, I'm staying for a couple of nights."

"We go to her favorite pancake breakfast place every year when she comes out for her birthday weekend," Rush said.

I turned to her. "Tomorrow is your birthday?"

"It's today, actually."

"Oh my gosh. Happy birthday!"

"Thank you. Rush had the chef make a special dinner for me. Salmon Oscar. It was very yummy."

It warmed my heart how protective and sweet he was being toward his mom. I really loved this side of Rush. If only he wasn't an insensitive prick the other half of the time.

He reached into his pocket and handed his mother a key. "Here. Take this and let yourself in."

She asked him, "Are you coming home tonight?"

Apparently, she knew her son enough to know that there was a chance he *wouldn't* be coming home. Probably figured he'd be staying at some skank's apartment.

"Yeah. I'm just gonna finish up some things here. I'll meet you back at the house. You can leave your art stuff here. I'll pack it all into my car and take it home."

"Thank you. Sounds good. I'm kind of looking forward to taking a hot bath." She turned and offered me a hug. "Gia...it was an absolute pleasure meeting you. You let me know when you'd like to come for a visit. I'll put on a pot of tea and block out the afternoon."

Embracing her, I said, "That sounds wonderful, Melody. Thank you. I plan on it. It was so great meeting you."

She started walking away, then stopped. "Actually, would you like to keep the painting I made tonight? I have so many. I can't keep them all."

"Oh my God. I would *love* to. Are you sure?"

"Totally. I would love for you to have it." She walked over to where it was and handed it to me.

"Thank you so much, Melody. Seriously, this really made my night. I'm gonna hang this up in my room."

I watched as she headed toward the stairs and disappeared. It was after closing, and Rush and I were now alone on the rooftop.

I held the painting in my hands, looking down at it. "Your mother is amazing."

"She is."

I placed the painting on a table then looked up at Rush for several seconds.

"What?" he asked. "You're looking at me funny."

"It's nothing."

"Let me guess...you're wondering how with my black heart and temper I can be so different from the kind and gentle, zen-filled soul that my mother is?"

"I didn't say that." I laughed.

"You were thinking it."

"No. I wasn't thinking that exactly, because I actually *do* think you're kind, too. Now I know where you get it from, that side of you. You've shown kindness to me. You just have a way of ruining it sometimes." I paused. "I want you to know that I apologized to your mother for my behavior earlier. And now, I'm apologizing to you."

"It's fine. You know...you only traumatized her because now she thinks her precious son is a butt burglar."

I burst into laughter. "Oh my God. Butt burglar?"

"Yeah, she's gonna have nightmares now." He winked.

"You're crazy."

We were both cracking up. At least, he didn't hate me anymore.

When the laughter died down, he said, "I'm sorry I lost control outside earlier."

I squinted at him. "No, you're not."

"You're right. I'd probably say that shit to you all over again."

"I figured."

"You made me mad talking to that pansy-ass bartender. I lost my mind a little."

"Well, if you don't want to be with me, you have to get used to seeing stuff like that."

"Doesn't mean I have to like it, especially when it's being thrown in front of me in my place of business."

Not wanting to get into it with him right now, I expelled a breath. "Can we just forget this entire night ever happened? Well, except for the part where I met your cool mother?"

He surprised me when he said, "Yeah. We can do that." Rush made his way over to the bar. "You want a night cap?"

"I'm driving home. I have Riley's car tonight, so I shouldn't drink."

He ignored me, grabbing a glass anyway. "I'll limit you to one, and I'll make it weak."

"What's the catch tonight? What expletive do I have to say to earn my free drink?"

"Babe...you alluded to ass fucking in front of my mom, I would say you're absolved for a while."

A shiver ran down my spine, and I couldn't figure it out if it was because of my embarrassment or the fact that he'd called me "babe."

I covered my mouth. "Oh my God. Did tonight really happen?"

"Afraid it did."

I watched in silence as he made some fruit concoction before slipping a little umbrella inside and sliding the glass toward me.

Taking a sip, I thought a bit more about how I immediately took to Melody. "Life is funny."

He cocked a brow. "Funny?"

"Yeah. I was just thinking about how we've both sort of experienced similar but opposite life situations. I have a great dad and no mother. And you have an awesome mom and no father. Well, you have a father... but you know what I mean."

He leaned into the bar and closed his eyes briefly. "Yeah, unfortunately, I do...know what you mean."

"Anyway, it's sort of something we have in common. When I was talking to your mom tonight, I found myself oddly envious of you, thinking that I would give anything to have a mother like her. Then, I had to remind myself that you're missing something, too."

Rush had been wiping the bar down but stopped and just looked at me.

I continued, "Anyway, I don't even know why I'm saying this to you right now. It's just—"

"I had the same thought when I met your dad."

It surprised me to hear him admit that. "Really?"

"Yeah. I remember thinking that I wouldn't have minded a cool cat like that for a father. So, you're not crazy. It's natural to feel envious. Sometimes you don't realize what you're missing until you see it right in front of you."

"Yeah. Exactly." He'd articulated my exact sentiments. "You're a complex soul, Rush."

I really wished I could've hung out here all night with him. Catching myself falling hard again when I was supposed to be working on getting over him, I suddenly forced myself up. "I really better get going."

Rush came around from behind the bar and stopped right in front of me. "Be careful on the road."

He was uncomfortably close, and his scent, the mixture of cigarettes and his signature cologne was making me weak. It reminded me of the night he spent in my bed. I was supposed to be leaving, but I hadn't moved. My nipples were tingling, and I had the sudden urge to answer his question from earlier.

"I've never had anyone come in through my back door, but I would be open to it with the right person. *Very* open."

Before I could capture his reaction, I slipped past him and headed for the stairs.

CHAPTER 12

Rush

I went to bed hard.

I woke up hard.

I was totally fucked.

There was no talking my dick down after those words exited Gia's mouth last night.

Very open.

Fuck. Me.

I needed to get myself in check before I had to go to breakfast with my mother.

After yet another jerk-off session in a long, cold shower, I finally made my way downstairs. I didn't even normally love jerking off. I much preferred being inside of an actual woman, but jerking off to thoughts of anal sex with Gia—well, that was just about the best I was gonna get aside from the real thing.

Mom was waiting for me in the kitchen when I finally emerged.

"Good morning, sleepyhead."

"Morning, Ma," I said, pouring some of the coffee she'd made.

"I wasn't sure if you were ever coming down."

"Yeah, I slept in. We should go eat. I'm starving."

Starving for Gia's ass.

"Actually, I wanted to wait for you to come down, but I can't go to breakfast. I have to get back home. I completely forgot my new couch is getting delivered this afternoon."

"Oh. Well, that sucks."

"Why don't you call Gia? Ask her to go to breakfast. I really like her."

"Ma..."

"Sit down, Heathcliff."

Fuck. My mother sitting me down and calling me by my given name was never a good sign. The last time she'd had me sit for a little one-on-one was when I was seventeen and she told me our dog died."

I pulled the chair out and planted my ass in it anyway.

"You know I rarely poke my nose into your private business."

And after last night's ass debauchery, I figured it would stay that way.

"I know..."

"You don't talk about women. In fact, pretty much the only time I even laid eyes on the women you...met... was when I saw them climbing out of your bedroom window in the middle of the night when you were a teenager."

My eyes widened. "You knew about that?"

She laughed. "Of course. And the water you filled my liquor bottles with to replace the alcohol you'd stolen.

And the first tattoo you got at sixteen, but didn't show me until you were eighteen. And all the times you rolled my car out of the driveway and borrowed it for the evening when I'd taken away your privileges for coming home late. By the way, I do appreciate you filling up the tank each time after you stole it."

I shook my head. "How come you never said anything about all that shit?"

"Because it's all part of growing up, sweetheart. I kept my eye on you from a distance to make sure you weren't going overboard or getting yourself into too much trouble. But I needed to let you live a little and experiment while you were under my roof. If you didn't start raising hell until you moved out, there would be no one to watch you. It's like those kids who drink for the first time when they go off to college. They're the ones who get hurt more than the kids who have experimented and learned their lessons already at home."

"Well...I'm not sure what to say. I'm sorry, I guess. For bringing girls home and being rotten."

My mother smiled. "That's not necessary. The point of my bringing this up to you now wasn't to make you feel bad or to have you apologize. It's to show you that while you might think you're hiding things from me, you're not always as good at it as you think."

"I'm not following you, Ma."

She reached over and patted my hand. "You have feelings for Gia. And she has them for you. Strong ones."

I raked a hand through my hair. "She's not a casual fu..." I caught myself just in time. "She's not someone you have a good time with and walk away from without hurting, Ma."

"So why do you need to walk away and hurt her?"

I opened my mouth to answer and realized I honestly didn't have one to give.

My mother offered me a sad smile. "Sweetheart, sometimes the risk of what bad things could happen keeps us from experiencing all the good things life has to offer."

My mother wasn't the type of person to throw out advice lightly. The best parts of me were the things that I learned by watching how she acted. So I contemplated what she'd said for a few minutes. I *wanted* to be with Gia...and not in the normal way I wanted to be with women—which usually capped out at a meal and a few hours in bed. I wanted to sit around and talk to her. I wanted to take her to my mother's to watch the way her eyes lit up when she looked at the paintings for the first time. Of course, I was also borderline obsessed with being inside her—not just getting her off and finishing myself off either. I wanted to fill every orifice of that damn woman. A few days ago, I'd dreamt of fucking that ballsy mouth of hers. Apparently yesterday it was ass day. So why *wasn't* I giving being together a chance?

There was only one answer, and I didn't like it very much at all.

I'm fucking afraid.

Coming to that realization, I looked up at my mother who'd been sitting there quietly just sipping her tea and waiting for me. Her eyes searched my face before she spoke again. "When you're afraid to fall in love with someone, it's usually because you've already started to fall, sweetheart."

And here I thought I was so slick all these years, keeping everything from my mother. I shook my head again. "Have you always been such a philosopher, and I didn't see it?"

She laughed. "Some of the best philosophers on love failed at love themselves, you know."

That broke my heart to hear my mother say. I knew my father had fucked her over, but I never really questioned why she didn't have a boyfriend most of my growing up. This was already a strange talk...what the fuck...

"How come you never dated when I was growing up?"

She sighed. "I actually really loved your father. He wasn't the person he is today when he was with me back then. At least he didn't seem to show me that side of him. Or I didn't want to see it. But I was blindsided when I found out he was married, and in that moment he revealed his true colors. It took me a long time to heal, and I was busy raising my beautiful son... working...painting. I used the excuse of being busy to justify not letting anyone in. You probably don't want to hear this...but I wasn't celibate all the years you were growing up, even though you never met anyone."

"You're right. I definitely don't want to hear that."

She smiled. "My outlook on relationships wasn't much better than yours is now. In fact, that's why it's so clear to me what's going on with you. It's like looking in the mirror at my life years ago in a lot of ways."

"And here you are giving me advice. Even though you don't take it yourself."

She got up and put her mug into the sink before sitting back down. "Actually, I have taken my own advice. I've been seeing someone."

My brows jumped. This was just getting fucking weird. "Oh yeah?"

"His name is Jeff. He's an art gallery curator. We've been seeing each other for almost a year now."

"A *year*? Why haven't you ever mentioned him? Or brought him with you on a visit?"

"I don't know. I guess in the beginning I assumed it would be my typical relationship. I hadn't expected it to blossom so beautifully."

Wow. Just wow.

"You're just opening up about everything today, aren't you?"

Mom laughed and stood. I took a close look at her for the first time in a long time. She looked really happy. "I need to get going for my couch delivery. If I miss it, they'll charge me another delivery fee. Why don't you and Gia come in next week one day and have lunch. I'll show her my work, and then we can all go over to Jeff's gallery and check out the show he has on display and have some dinner. I think it's time you meet him."

She walked to me, and I stood and enveloped her in a big hug. I had an ache in my chest when the thought that Gia didn't have a mother to do this with popped into my head. It made me want to share mine with her.

"I'll load your car for you."

Watching Mom drive away, I waved one last time when I caught her looking back at me in the rearview mirror. I stood at the bottom of my driveway for a few minutes just thinking. Until it hit me. Had I just set up a double date with my mother—and a woman I wasn't dating?

———

I was fake repairing a car...*this was a first*.

While I ignored my mother's suggestion of taking Gia to breakfast, I decided to use the day to pretend to fix Gia's car—the car I'd already fixed and never told her about. The car I'd repaired and then lost a bet to have a reason to do the repairs I'd already done. Anything that had to do with this woman wound up being a little fucking nutty for some reason.

But here I was, with a Nissan jacked up in the air while I lay beneath it listening to music and pretending to do shit. I'd knocked on the door and gotten Gia's keys, feigning that they were necessary to fix the brakes and tire. Luckily, the combo of serious shit I talked about with my mother this morning and whacking off seemed to keep me from embarrassing myself when she answered the door groggy eyed, wearing a skimpy pair of shorts and a tank top with no fucking bra on.

I'd told her I'd come to pay my bet debt and needed to get started so I could head over to the construction site at one of my properties. But the truth was, the crew wasn't working on Saturday. I just wanted to head off her inviting me to stay or anything. My head was still spinning from my conversation with my mother, and I wasn't in the right frame of mind to spend time with Gia.

About a half-hour into my fake repair, I felt a tap at my leg so I climbed out from under the car.

Fuck me.

I couldn't even attempt to hide the way I leered. Gia was standing next to the car wearing a yellow bikini and holding what looked like two glasses of iced tea. Her ample tits were perky as all fuck and the little bikini top barely covered her areolas.

"What the hell are you wearing?" I finally growled.

She looked down. "A bathing suit. It's beautiful out, so I'm going to lie out by the pool for an hour or two before starting to write."

"That's not a bathing suit, those are scraps of a bathing suit that someone shredded."

She tilted her head. "Are you saying you don't like it?"

"Do you wear that in public?"

"Not usually. I only wear it in the yard because it's so skimpy. But it's perfect for tanning."

"Good." I grabbed the tea from her hand without asking and chugged it down. Today was warm, but suddenly I was starting to sweat. "Thanks for the tea. You should go back into the yard before you get cited for indecent exposure."

She narrowed her eyes at me. "You're a jerk."

"Yes. I know that. You've made that clear. To me... and my mother."

She pouted. "Are you going to make me feel bad about that forever?"

I grinned. "Probably."

Gia stuck her tongue out at me. *God, I want to see that thing lick the head of my cock.*

I sat down on the driveway, readying to lie back and finish up my pretend repair. "Don't stick that thing out, unless you plan to use it, little girl."

"I'll be by the pool if you need me."

I crawled back under the car. "Fine."

Of course, that wasn't the end of it. This was Gia I was dealing with. "Rush."

I crawled back out. "What?"

A sinful little smile spread across her face. "Just didn't want you to miss my walking back to the house. *Considering your obsession with my ass lately.*"

Before I could respond, she turned to walk away, revealing the backside of her bathing suit. Or more correctly, the lack of a backside to her bathing suit. Gia was wearing a thong bottom that revealed two perfectly round globes, and those babies were fucking taunting me as they jiggled their way up toward the house.

"*Jesus H. Christ,*" I grumbled to myself. I'd never given any thought to what the H stood for before, but at that point, with how he was testing my patience, I was pretty sure it was *heartless.*

———

"All done." I found Gia in the yard sunbathing. Of course, she had to be lying on her stomach so I could get a closer look at her ass. It was fucking phenomenal. Like a chubby, upside-down heart from where I stood. I'd spent the last hour pretend fixing her car and picturing her riding me reverse cowgirl, those ass cheeks jiggling like fucking Jell-O while she rode me hard. I had to force my eyes to her face and clear my throat to continue. "Here are your keys. Your rotors were shot, too. In the future, don't ride on bad brakes. It just turns a little problem into a big one."

She shielded her eyes from the sun and twisted her neck to look up at me, still not flipping over to her stomach. "Oh. Okay. Thanks. Can I make you some lunch? It's the least I can do to repay you for hours of working on my car."

Is that ass on the menu?

"No. I have to get going."

She lifted from flat on her stomach to on her knees in a yoga-like pose, taking her sweet ass time before turning over.

"Are you sure?" She bit her bottom lip. "You've had to have worked up an appetite."

Is she fucking with me? I had an appetite alright. "I gotta run."

I sounded like a broken record, yet here I still stood. My head wanted to get the fuck out of that yard, but my traitorous feet wouldn't move. Not even when she stood up, turned around and practically rubbed her ass against me as she held up suntan lotion. "Could you rub some sunscreen on my back before you go? I don't want to burn."

No. "Sure."

"Thanks."

I took the sunscreen and squeezed a glob of creamy white lotion into the palm of my hand. Swallowing hard, I began to rub it into her back. Her shoulders were warm and soft with the tiniest little layer of fuzz on it. It reminded me of a peach. My mouth salivated at the thought of biting into her.

"Could you do a little lower?"

My breathing became labored and my cock swelled as I lowered my hands and rubbed into the middle of her back. I was breaching into dangerous territory.

"Lower" she said. I knew from her breathy voice that I wasn't the only one aroused.

I lowered to just above her bathing suit bottom and rubbed lotion all over.

When I finished, she turned her head so I could see the side of her face and closed her eyes to whisper, "lower."

Fuck me.

I couldn't stop myself. I reached for the creamy sunscreen and squeezed enough into my hand to cover a large person's full body and then began to rub it into her ass cheeks. She had the most unique heart-shaped mole on her left side that was perfectly symmetrical. I ran my fingertips over it. When I trailed a pool of lotion to the top of her ass crack, and slowly rubbed it in tracing the material of her bathing suit in between her cheeks, she let out a low moan.

More. Make more sounds like that.

All I could think about was how I wanted to bend her over and fuck her from behind. I wanted to mark every inch of the perfect skin on her shoulders with my teeth while I tunneled so far inside of her that I'd never come out again. My heart raced out of control when she took a step back and pressed her body against mine. But...I didn't want it this way. She wasn't some fuck you bent over in the yard before giving the neighbors a good show.

"*Gia...*" My voice shook while I tried to stop what was two seconds away from happening."

Luckily, a woman's voice broke through the haze of lust that mine couldn't crack. Only it wasn't Gia's. Turning my head in a fog, I realized it was her roommate, Riley, who worked for me.

Fuck.

"*Uh.* Sorry. I didn't realize anyone was with you," she yelled.

On instinct, I jumped back.

Riley disappeared into the house, and in the seconds that it took Gia to turn around, I snapped myself out of it.

"Sorry about that," she said. "You ready to rub the rest in?"

"I gotta go." It was the third time I'd said it, but this time I meant it. I practically tripped over the bottle of sunscreen at my feet trying to get the fuck out of there.

Gia yelled, "Rush. *Wait.*"

But I didn't stop until I was inside of my car. I had no idea why I was running away like a coward, but it felt like I was doing Gia a favor.

CHAPTER 13

Gia

Another day wasted. No writing. No plotting. *Nothing* accomplished.

And I had a burn on my ass from the hours I'd spent lying on my stomach waiting for Rush to walk into the yard. I'd never worn a thong bathing suit in my life. Which was why my sun-virgin ass cheeks felt like they were on fire.

When Rush showed up this morning, I'd snuck into Riley's room and grabbed one of her skimpy suits. I still couldn't believe I'd had the nerve to wear the thing—it barely covered my breasts and exposed my entire ass.

But not even practically throwing myself at him naked worked. It made me feel depressed and more than a little angry. Riley noticed and came to sit with me on the couch.

"Spill your guts, four eyes."

I switched sitting positions for the millionth time today, leaning more on my left hip than the burn, and pushed my glasses up onto my head. "I have no idea how you wear that bathing suit. My ass is fried to a crisp."

"Oh no you don't. You're not avoiding this conversation anymore by blaming your depressing face on a burned ass."

"What do you mean?"

She shot me a look that said *no more bullshitting me*. "What's going on with you and the boss? I saw him out there with you this morning, rubbing lotion into your ass. It looked like he was about to squirt a different cream on you."

"He came over to fix my car. I practically threw myself at him. *Again*. But nothing happened."

"I honestly have no idea what you see in him. Well, aside from the obvious—that he's fucking hot. But he's such a douche."

I shook my head. "He's not really. Not once you get to know him. I think it's his way of keeping people at a distance. He definitely doesn't let people in easily."

"But he let you in?"

"I think so, yes. We have a connection. I know he's attracted to me. And I'm most definitely attracted to him. But it's more than that. Although none of that does me any good because he won't let anything happen between us physically, no matter how hard I try. I don't get it."

Riley pointed a finger. "You just answered your own question."

"What are you talking about?"

"You said you two have a connection that's more than physical."

"So?"

"That's the problem."

"I'm not following."

"A guy like Rush is a love 'em and leave 'em type of guy. I've worked at The Heights for three years. He has a certain type that he goes out with."

I rolled my eyes. "Yes. *Whorey*. I've seen a few stop in."

"There's a reason he only gets involved with a certain type of woman."

"What is it?"

Riley laughed. "I don't know. But you probably do if you've gotten close like you said." She shrugged. "Maybe an ex burned him."

"I don't think he's had any long-term relationships."

"Okay." She tapped her finger to her lip. "It's not a relationship that someone is usually afraid of, it's *a bad* relationship. And that usually comes from something in their life, like an ex. But maybe it's something different."

His father.

*And how his father treated his mothe*r. That could've given him a negative outlook for sure. But I didn't want to discuss Rush's private business with Riley, even though I considered her a good friend.

"I'm not sure. But if that's the case, and he avoids relationships because of something in his life, how would I even get past that?"

Riley tossed a throw pillow she had been holding on her lap at me. "You don't, silly. You give him what he *thinks* he wants, and let the relationship happen naturally. Tell him you just want a fuck buddy for the summer. Set his mind at ease that he doesn't need to worry about the relationship part. Start humping each other, and if it's meant to be, the rest will just fall into place, and he won't even realize it until it's too late."

"I don't know...that sounds like someone could get hurt..."

"Yes. *You.* If after your fuck buddy time is over, he breaks it off, of course you're going to be hurt. But what do you have now? A weird friendship and celibacy. Look, when you leave after the summer is over, you're going to be crushed if he doesn't want to keep in touch, right? So why not have a bangin' summer—pun intended—if you're going to be sulking in September anyway?"

I suppose she had a point...there was just one problem. "But Rush doesn't see me that way."

"So make him see you that way."

"How?"

"How long until you have to work?"

I looked at my phone. "About an hour and a half."

Riley stood. "Come on, that's not a lot of time to turn your nice ass into a whore."

———

I felt like the pink ladies had just turned me into sexy Sandy from *Grease*. Getting out of my car, I looked down at my outfit one last time and took a deep breath. Red, low-cut shirt, short skirt, and heels that I doubted I could last an hour in, no less working all night. Riley had added a ton of body to my naturally wavy hair and done my makeup with all that contour stuff that I see people doing on YouTube, but never bothered to try out.

I glanced at my reflection in the window as I walked toward the door. I looked good. Sexy, in a slutty kind of way. Definitely more like the women Rush went out with. Oak whistled and opened the door. "Looking good, Gia."

I blushed, but his comment actually helped my confidence level a little. "Thank you."

Inside, I looked around, and a rush of relief washed over me finding no sign of the boss. Dressing for the part was only half the plan. I needed to actually cough up the courage to approach Rush and offer him...well, *my body*.

I threw myself into my usual prep before dinner—going over the reservations, checking in with the kitchen on what the specials are so that I knew them when people called and asked—they *always* called ahead and asked—bringing the bars extra bottles of whatever liquor was in the drink special of the evening, and helping the busboys set up the tables. I'd been there about an hour, with no sign of Rush still. It lulled me into feeling at ease, thinking maybe he wouldn't show up tonight, and I wouldn't have the chance to make my proposal to him.

Which was why when I opened the door to the back office to put one of the cordless phones on the charger, I didn't expect anyone to be inside.

I jumped finding Rush. His desk was unusually clear, and he was sitting there staring off into space. "Rush! Sorry. I didn't think you were here yet."

His eyes made a slow sweep down my body and an even slower ascent. They snagged on my abundant cleavage on display for long seconds before his gaze met mine. "All dressed up tonight for a reason?"

Shit.

He'd just handed me the perfect opportunity to open the door. I swallowed and tried not to squirm. "Yes."

Rush's eyes narrowed. "Date?"

"Maybe."

His stare was intense. "Who's the lucky guy?"

My pulse started to race. It was about to happen. *Don't chicken out, Gia. Don't be a chicken shit all your life.*

Rush stood from his desk and walked around it. The office wasn't very big to begin with, but having him two feet away while I said what I wanted to say made it feel like the walls were closing in on me.

He folded his arms and his jaw ticked. "Who'd you put that slutty outfit on for, Gia?"

I looked down at my feet, took a deep breath, and then met his gaze head on. "You. I wore this outfit for you."

Rush took a step closer. His face was hard, not giving anything away. "You like to wear skimpy things for me, don't you?"

I nodded.

"You like to tease me?"

My palms started to sweat. "No. Well, yes. But I don't want to tease you anymore."

He tilted his head. "You're done teasing me?"

"Yes."

"But you wore that outfit anyway?"

"Yes."

"You don't understand the definition of teasing then?"

Spit it out, Gia. Spit it out!

I took one last deep breath. I was either going to hyperventilate or get through this. "Teasing is when you provoke someone with no intention of following through." I looked into his eyes. "I'd like to follow through. I think you and me...*we should have sex.*" Now that I'd popped the cork off the bottle, words started to pour out of me. "You don't do relationships. We're obviously attracted to each other. Sometimes we get along...although sometimes we fight, too. But it's summer and...you know...we both have needs. So why not just be fuck buddies?" I cringed after that last part I said, thinking I sounded like a whore. Or Riley. *Well...*Riley *did* sleep around a lot. But that was beside the point. Now I couldn't stop the rambling in my head, much less the rambling of my mouth. *Great. Just great.*

Rush arched a brow. "Fuck buddies?"

I pinched my come-fuck-me red painted lips shut and nodded.

"You only want to fuck me then? Nothing more?"

I nodded.

"I see." He stared at me. "Let me get this straight... so we're clear. You don't want to date me?"

"No."

"But you want to fuck me?"

"Yes."

"So I could say...pop over to your place after work anytime I wanted and maybe eat you out?"

I swallowed. "Yes."

"And maybe sometimes you'd give me a blow job."

"Sure."

"And I could leave after sex was over? No snuggling or niceties required?"

"That's right."

His damn face was so stoic; I had no clue what was going on in that head of his. After another minute-long, intense stare that I almost crumbled under, he walked back behind his desk and took a seat.

"How long do I have?"

"Pardon?"

"To decide and give you my answer to your proposal."

"Oh." I hadn't thought that far. But I couldn't torture myself forever. I straightened my spine. "By the end of the night."

Rush picked up a pen and pulled a piece of paper from a neat pile on the corner of his desk. Beginning to read, he grumbled without looking up. "Go back to fucking work, Gia."

———

The rest of that night was tense, to say the least.

I'd catch Rush staring at me while I worked. He wasn't flirting or anything. In fact, he looked more pissed as the night wore on. It was impossible to know what he was thinking.

Unable to concentrate, I was making mistakes left and right, forgetting to bring menus to the table or leading people to the wrong sections—all of this, of course, under Rush's watchful eye.

The realization of what I'd done was starting to hit me. Why had I gotten dressed up like this? The man had officially driven me to act crazy. I'd made a fool of myself in front of him—thrown myself at him. That was never the answer to getting a man to want you. That was the opposite of what someone should do.

I'd gotten myself glammed up, made myself look like a slut, even though, deep down, I knew his attraction to me was never the issue; it was that he didn't *want* to be with me. Period. He liked messing with me, flirting with me, pushing the limits. But he didn't actually want to pull the trigger. If he did, it would have happened by now. I had mistaken his alpha male need to protect me for serious interest. I was dead wrong. The man had issues, and I was done with being one of them.

At one point, with about an hour left until closing, Rush brushed by me and said, "Come to my office after your shift." He walked away before I could respond, leaving the musky scent of cigarettes and cologne in his wake.

Great. This was it. This was going to be the point where he gave me all of the reasons why he didn't want to pursue anything with me.

He knew that I wasn't the sex-only type. We'd talked about that very fact, for Christ's sake. There was no tricking him.

Besides, why would he bother with someone who was emotionally needy when he had beautiful women falling at his feet all of the time, ones who truly only wanted the same thing he did? Just sex, not love.

You're such a fool, Gia.

After my shift ended, I kept putting off going to his office. He'd disappeared from the main area, so I assumed he might have been waiting for me back there.

Maybe I'd ditch him and just go home. After all, I had a functioning car parked right outside now, thanks to him. There was no reason I had to put myself through the agony of hearing his rejection.

I kept stalling until he finally marched down to the hostess area, looking more pissed-off than ever.

"We closed a half-hour ago. I thought I told you to meet me in my office. I've been waiting there for you."

Organizing some menus and no longer looking him in the eye, I said, "Yeah, well, I don't have to jump just because you tell me to."

"Gia..." he barked. When I looked up, his eyes seared into mine. "Get your ass in my office."

Rush stormed away, and I gave in, following him with my heart pounding.

After shutting the door behind me, I folded my arms. "Okay, what?"

Rush sat down and kicked his feet up on the desk. He began tapping a pen repeatedly before saying, "I've been thinking about what you proposed earlier, and I don't think it's a good idea. I—"

"Stop!" I yelled. I was losing it. "Just stop! I don't need to hear this, okay? I already know what you're going to say, that you don't believe I really meant what I said about being friends with benefits. You'll never view me as a fuck buddy. Yada Yada. Please spare me. I don't need to sit through the explanation."

His rolling chair banged against the back wall as he suddenly got up. After marching toward where I was standing, he stopped about a foot away from me. "Will you let me finish?"

I backed away from him toward the door. "No. I don't want to talk about it. I acted like a fool, throwing myself at you, and it never should've happened. You're right. I'm not the type of girl for you. I have dignity and self-respect, and I want more—so much more than to be your fuck toy. I don't care how attractive you are with all of that mysterious, bad-boy shit you have going on. In the end, you're a man who wants none of the same things that I do out of life."

"Can I just—"

"No," I interrupted. "I'm gonna go."

Just as I turned around, I felt his hand grip my wrist. He flipped me around before backing me up against the door.

I could feel his breath as he spoke close to my face. "You are so fucking stubborn. I should bend you over and smack your ass so hard for not letting me get a word in edgewise."

My nipples went erect upon that thought. I swallowed. "See...this is what you do. You—"

"Shut. Up."

Before I could ream him out for telling me to shut up, his lips were on mine, swallowing up all of my unsaid, smartass comments. My legs nearly collapsed from the sheer power of his kiss.

Rush's hands were buried in my hair as he pushed his tongue inside my mouth. I desperately met the rhythm of its thrusts. He tasted so damn good, like cigarettes and a taste all his own. I moaned into his mouth, unable to hide my desperation for more. My hands were now digging through his hair, pressing his lips deeper into mine. I couldn't get enough of his intoxicating taste.

His scruff burned a little against my chin as he leaned his body farther into mine and continued to invade my mouth. He ran his hands from my hair all the way down my back until they landed on my ass. He squeezed it hard before unapologetically pushing his rigid cock against my abdomen.

His low grumbles of pleasure were all I'd imagined them to be. I felt myself falling weaker and weaker the more he continued to devour my lips. My panties were now soaked, and I knew I was a goner if he tried to take me right then and there.

Rush sucked on my bottom lip hard before suddenly ripping himself away. He looked pained as he panted. "We need to talk."

CHAPTER 14

Rush

Gia looked like I'd pissed in her Cheerios after I stopped the kiss.

Pulling away from that was one of the hardest things I'd ever had to do. But we needed to have this discussion. Not to mention, I wasn't going to fuck her in my office. It was heading dangerously close to that scenario. A few more seconds of that kiss, and I wasn't sure if I would have been able to stop.

She was gasping for air. "What do you need to say?"

My dick was still hard as a rock as I said, "If you had stopped talking for two seconds earlier, you'd realize that you were wrong about what you *thought* I was going to tell you tonight."

Deep breath.

I continued, "I don't want to just fuck..." I corrected my language, because what I had to say was important. "Don't want to just...*sleep* with you." Letting out a breath, I pushed the rest of the words out, "I think we should...see where things go."

Her jaw dropped. "What are you getting at?"

"Earlier when you walked into my office all made up, looking like freaking Betty Boop, I was in the middle of thinking about this thing with us, trying to figure out my feelings. But there wasn't anything to figure out except that I've been in denial. I can't promise you anything, Gia. I can't promise that I'm not gonna fuck this up royally. But...I wanna try."

Her eyes widened in genuine surprise. "You want more than just a casual fuck with me?"

I nodded. "Yeah." Moving in, I wrapped my hands around her cheeks and rubbed some of the remaining lipstick away from her mouth. "And you don't need all that shit on your face. You're so fucking beautiful without it. Next time you do that, I'm gonna kiss it all off of you."

"Is that a challenge?" A blush crept up her face. "So...what we do now? Where do we go from here?"

The concept of dating was so foreign to me. I couldn't remember the last time I'd taken a woman out on a formal date. The slower I took things with Gia, the less chance I had of screwing things up. That meant avoiding being alone with her for a while.

"You're off tomorrow night, right?" I asked.

"Yeah."

"I'll come get you."

She smirked. "You're taking me out on a date?"

My heart started to palpitate at the thought. "Look...I don't really know what I'm doing when it comes to *dating*. I haven't been on an actual date in a very long time. But yeah, I'll pick you up. Take you out."

"Pick me up. Take me out. That's sounds a lot like a *date* to me," she teased.

I rolled my eyes, then smiled in concession. "Alright, damn it. It's a date."

———

What's wrong with me tonight?

Indecisive as hell, I took off the third shirt I'd put on in five minutes and threw it in the corner of my bedroom. You'd think I'd never taken a woman out before.

I wasn't used to dressing up, either, finally settling on a charcoal collared shirt and dark jeans.

The reality was, the right shirt wasn't going to protect me from my own self-destructive behavior tonight. I knew damn well I had no control over my physical reaction to Gia. Yes, I wanted to get to know her even better. Yes, I wanted to hang out with her. But I wanted to fuck her more than my next breath, and I worried that the minute we started touching again tonight, that need would trump all. I was gonna lose it. I just knew it.

I'd made a reservation for us at a posh seafood restaurant about a half-hour away. I figured the longer the drive, the better. That was more time in the car where I couldn't get myself into trouble on the very first night of "dating."

The sun was just starting to set as I pulled up to the beach house.

After I rang the doorbell, I wiped the sweat off my forehead as I waited for her to answer. The fact that she still didn't know I owned her damn place made me chuckle to myself.

Gia opened, looking good enough to eat right there on the spot, and that only confirmed how fucked I was. She was wearing a low-cut yellow dress that was long and flowy. Even though it was sexy, it didn't come across as slutty. She wore her hair down in waves. This sparkly headband sat atop her head and across her forehead. It reminded me of something Cleopatra would have worn. Gia was naturally exotic and beautiful, so I was glad she'd listened to me and kept the makeup to a minimum. She didn't need it.

"You look nice." I smiled.

"So do you," she said.

Not knowing what the fuck to do with them, I slipped my hands into my pockets. I'd become conscious of my every movement. It was like I suddenly forgot how to act around her. Now that we knew where things stood and I had free reign to touch her, I was scared shitless that I was going to move too fast and do something to hurt her.

As we made our way back to my Mustang, she asked, "Where are we going?"

"You ever hear of Oceanside Manor?"

"Yes. That place is crazy fancy."

"Try to behave, then." I winked, opening up the passenger side door. "No breaking up any brawls tonight."

As she settled into the seat, she took a deep breath in. "I've missed riding in your car."

Damn, I've missed it, too.

She crossed her legs, revealing that the dress she was wearing had a massive slit that allowed me a view of her toned and tanned leg all the way up to the top of her thigh.

Damn. Damn. Damn. So much for extra time in the car keeping me out of trouble.

Reaching into my pocket for a cigarette, I realized I'd run out. There was no way I was gonna survive a thirty-minute ride with "legs" over here if I couldn't smoke.

Down the road, I abruptly stopped at a 7-Eleven before we had to get on the highway.

"What are you doing?"

"I have to get some smokes. I left my pack at home."

I ran out of the car fast so I didn't have to hear her guilt trip about the fact that I was still smoking. Tonight was not the night to quit.

"Pack of Marlboro," I said to the cashier.

When he rang me up, I reached into my pocket for my wallet to find that it wasn't there. Patting my clothing down, I soon figured out that I'd left my wallet at home.

Shit!

I'd been so preoccupied with my wardrobe like a pussy, I forgot the most important thing.

Leaning against the counter, I let out a long breath and slid the cigarettes back toward the man.

"Sorry, dude. Forgot my wallet."

Gia must have sensed the pissed look on my face when I returned to the car.

"What's wrong?"

Cranking the ignition, I sighed. "We have to go back. I left my wallet at home. We'll just stop by my place, and I'll run in and get it."

She placed her hand on my thigh, and it made my dick stir. "Don't be silly. I can pay for dinner."

There was no freaking way I was going to let Gia do that, even if I paid her back. I couldn't imagine anything more humiliating than watching her open her wallet tonight and pay the tab.

"Nah. I'll head back."

The entire ride to my house, I was bracing myself for her reaction when we pulled into my driveway. She'd never seen where I lived.

As we finally approached—as predicted—her eyes bugged out of her head when she got a load of my digs.

"Oh my God. *This* is your house? It's amazing."

Even though I didn't blow money like my father and brother, with the riches I'd inherited, the one thing I'd afforded myself was a damn nice place of residence.

Two levels, all glass windows on the exterior, and overlooking the ocean, it was definitely a sweet property. There was no denying that. It was on a small private area of beach, secluded—just the way I liked it.

I was just about to run in when Gia asked, "Do you mind if I go in with you? I'd love to see the inside."

It shouldn't have surprised me that she wanted to see the house. Technically, I should've been a gentleman and invited her in. I just didn't trust myself alone with her. But what was I supposed to do now, make her stay in the car after she'd asked to see it?

"Yeah. Sure."

Once inside, Gia looked around, soaking in my modern but minimalist style. Most of my furniture was black or gray. The walls of the main space were white and covered in my mother's paintings. I'd specifically asked her to paint different variations of the moon over the ocean at night.

Gia was soaking it all in. "Rush...this place. It's..."

"Thank you."

It didn't take her long to notice the artwork. She walked straight over to the portrait of the fullest moon. "Did your mother do these?"

I trailed behind her. "Yes."

"They're amazing," she said brushing her finger gently over the canvas. "Do you have an obsession with the moon?"

"You could say I like the moon, yeah. He's always there for me and has a little bit of a dark side, like I do, I suppose. I asked my mother to paint different interpretations of the moon over the water at night."

I could tell the wheels were turning in Gia's head, like she was trying to figure out the meaning behind why I loved the moon, maybe trying to find some correlation between it and my yearning for dependability or love or some shit.

"Well, I definitely think the moon suits you over the sun."

I cocked a brow. "Because I'm a lunatic?"

She laughed. "Well, yeah, but also just the dark, mysterious vibe."

Gia just kept wandering around the house, oblivious to my itch to leave. "Do you mind if I check out the second level?"

I wasn't going to be able to get out of this, but a part of me was starting to want to show her more as I became used to having her inside my home. Instead of answering, I nudged my head and led her to follow me up the stairs.

She waltzed through my bedroom and burst open the doors that led to the upper deck.

The last of the sun was going down over the breezy ocean. Gia just stood there soaking in the evening air and the scenery. She looked exquisite with her hair blowing around as she gazed out at the water.

We were both quiet for a long while, listening to the seagulls before she finally spoke.

"If I lived here, I'm pretty sure I would never leave."

An image of Gia in shackles, tied to my bed, unable to leave, flashed through my brain.

Can't help your thoughts, right?

When she turned to me, for some reason, I got the urge to say, "You're really pretty. You know that?"

Where did that come from?

"I bet you say that to all the girls you bring up to this balcony."

I rarely brought women home if I could help it. Typically, I'd go to their place. On the rare occasions that I couldn't avoid it, I never took them up to my private bedroom, which led to this balcony. I'd use the first-floor guest bedroom to "entertain."

"You're the first girl who's ever stood on it."

Her forehead wrinkled. "Are you serious?"

"Yes. I'm a private guy. I've never brought a woman up here before. This...the upstairs...is like my sanctuary."

"How come you let me up here, then?"

"Fuck if I know. I guess...I trust you...or something."

Her brow lifted. "Or something?"

"Something I don't even understand. I lose my mind around you. From the second I met you, you set something off in me that I haven't been able to contain."

"So, don't...contain it."

I inched closer to her, placing a piece of hair behind her ear. "It's like I want to protect you and corrupt you at the same time. It's fucked-up."

"It's not fucked-up. It's sweet."

"You wouldn't think it was sweet if you knew what was going on in my head right now."

"I think I have a vague idea."

Wanting to kiss her so badly, I held back, instead looking down at my phone. "We should get going..."

"Did you have a dinner reservation?"

"Yeah. We missed it."

She looked hesitant to say, "Do you mind if we hang out here instead of going there? I'm not really in the mood to go to a restaurant. I feel like I spend half my life in one. I would love to just sit out on this deck with a glass of wine. Maybe get some takeout?"

That sounded like exactly what I'd want to do if I weren't so damn scared to be alone with her.

When I didn't answer, she said, "It's okay if you'd prefer not to."

"No. It's fine," I spit out. "We can stay here."

My night just got a whole lot more challenging.

CHAPTER 15

Gia

Rush had ordered Italian from a restaurant called Margarita's that was down the road from him.

We'd had some wine with our eggplant parmesan and shrimp scampi. He seemed a lot more relaxed than he had been earlier.

There was a kickass patio set up on the upper deck. We were both lying out on two separate outdoor chaise lounges. He was sipping his wine and smoking as his hair blew around in the night breeze. It was dark out now, making the flicker of his cigarette ash more prominent.

He'd kept a good two feet away from me all night. But I couldn't help wishing he would move closer as the memory of our kiss from yesterday consumed my thoughts. I'd never been kissed so forcefully, so passionately. I could only imagine how he was in bed.

Over dinner, we'd talked about a lot of things, including our childhoods and a little about his various businesses. We'd managed to cover the gamut—well, besides the subject of what exactly was happening between us.

Now, we were just staring out at the ocean again.

"I feel so calm here. It's just so peaceful," I said.

"I've never shared this view with anyone."

"I still can't believe that."

He put out his cigarette before reaching out his hand to me. "I like having you here. A lot."

I squeezed it, noticing a look of worry on his face. "You look like that troubles you a little. What's wrong with liking that?

He was silent for the longest time before he said, "Don't put up with any shit from me, Gia. Alright?"

"What is that supposed to mean?"

"If you catch me starting to fuck up, put me in my place."

It was clear that Rush had some deep-rooted fears about hurting me. Maybe it stemmed from his father abandoning his mother.

"You know, I could hurt *you* just as bad as you could hurt me. Remember, I'm the daughter of a woman who abandoned her husband and daughter. I could have bad blood in me, too. But I'm not gonna worry about it. And I'm not afraid of you, Rush."

"You should be."

"Why?"

"Because I want to do really bad things to you right now. What I really should be doing is taking you home."

"I don't want to leave."

His eyes were piercing. "What *do* you want, Gia?"

Feeling bold, I lifted myself out of my seat, crawled over to his lounger, and began to straddle him. "This," I said before devouring his lips and kissing him with every ounce of my soul. "I want you, Rush," I whispered over his lips.

The speed of the kiss accelerated as he suddenly lifted me up off the chair, carrying me through the doors to his bed.

He put me down, hovering over me. "I want to go slow, but I really need to taste your pussy, Gia."

His words made the muscles between my legs pulsate.

Rush slowly lifted the skirt of my dress, burying his head between my legs. He softly kissed the skin between my thighs.

I wriggled, unable to control my body's reaction to the sensation.

"Relax," he said.

When his tongue hit my clit, I swore I saw stars. Letting out a squeal from the contact, I bent my head back in ecstasy. My legs were now trembling.

He pulled me closer in one harsh movement, as he buried his mouth in me, lapping his tongue over my clit and using his entire mouth to pleasure me.

My eyes were closed as I felt his fingers slip inside me. He was finger-fucking me as he continued to devour my flesh.

I didn't expect to come so fast. My muscles just started to contract over his mouth. I lasted all of about a minute, unable to remember the last time a man had used his mouth to pleasure me.

I screamed out in climax as I pulled on Rush's hair.

He'd left me completely limp and speechless. Coming up for air, Rush licked his lips and groaned, "I can't wait to fuck you, Gia."

His erection was straining through his jeans. I knew he needed release, and I couldn't wait to give it to him.

Grabbing onto his belt buckle, I tried to unzip his pants when he placed his hand over mine to stop me.

"I can't go there tonight. I'll wreck you." He suddenly hopped off the bed. "I'll be right back."

He disappeared for a long while, and when he came back, I could only assume he'd gone to jerk off, because he seemed calm.

"Scoot over," he said as he enveloped me in his arms.

He'd given me the best orgasm of my life, and now he was holding me. I couldn't say it got any better than that.

"I missed this," I said. "Sleeping next to you."

"You only had it once and you missed it?" he said against my back.

"Every night since."

Rush kissed my back softly. "Me, too, Gia."

The warmest feeling came over me. I felt incredibly safe in his arms, safer than I probably ever had in my entire life

He traced his fingers up and down my arm as he lay behind me, spooning. Relaxed and content in the moment, I closed my eyes to enjoy the post orgasmic haze that blanketed me.

Our chests moving in unison, his front to my back, must have rocked me to sleep. Because the next thing I knew, the warmth of the sun hitting my face woke me to find an empty bed.

I leaned against the kitchen doorway. Now *that* was a morning view I could get used to.

Rush stood in front of the oven, shirtless with his hair wet, cooking something that smelled delicious while swaying to music. It struck me as odd that the music was country. I'd have taken him more for heavy metal or something.

"You gonna stand there and stare at me, or come give me a kiss good morning?" Rush spoke without turning around.

"How did you know I was even standing here?"

He rapped his knuckles on the stainless-steel hood over the oven. "Reflection. Nice outfit, by the way."

I'd fallen asleep in my dress, and when I saw the shirt Rush wore yesterday on the floor next to the bed this morning, I decided to change into it after washing up in his bathroom.

I padded over to him and wrapped my arms around his waist. "Good morning."

He craned his neck back and met my tilted head for a kiss. "Sleep good?"

"Actually, really good. I don't even remember falling asleep. Your bed must be really comfortable."

He chuckled. "Yeah. It was the bed, not my mouth on your pussy that tuckered you out."

"You're so crass."

He plated the eggs in the pan just as toast popped up from the toaster. "I forgot, I have to bribe you with a drink to get you to say dirty words." He winked. "Go sit. I'll make you some coffee and decide what I want to hear in order for you to get any caffeine."

We sat down together for breakfast, and I couldn't help but ogle Rush's body. He had a lean, yet strong, muscular build. His pecs were sculpted, abs were chiseled into a six pack—or maybe it was eight—I definitely wanted to count the peaks and valleys with my tongue at some point, and his arms were corded and bulged each time he brought his coffee mug to his lips. I won't even get started on that thin line of hair that ran from his bellybutton down into his sweatpants.

"What's going on in that nutty head of yours this morning?" Rush had been watching me stare.

"I'm just checking out the merchandise."

He arched a brow.

"What? You got to see me before you decided to ask me out on a date. I didn't get to see you."

His brows drew down. "When did I get to see you naked?"

"In the yellow bikini."

He smirked. "That wasn't exactly naked. Although I did see some areola and your entire ass. So it was pretty close."

I don't know what it was about Rush, but he made me bold. I shot him a devilish grin. "Well, I wouldn't want to be unfair." I promptly lifted the shirt I had on up and over my head, tossing it on the floor. I'd left my bra with my dress in the bedroom, so all I had on was a black lacey thong.

Rush's fork clanked to the plate. "*Fuck.*" He swallowed. "You're not making this easy."

I tilted my head coyly. "Are you saying, I make it *hard* for you?"

His eyes trained on my breasts. I actually watched them darken to a deeper shade of green. "You have gorgeous tits."

"Thank you." I sipped my coffee, trying to act casual.

"I'd like to fuck them."

I choked mid-sip and sputtered some coffee onto my plate. I'd started this, but Rush had certainly taken over. My mouth was suddenly dry, and it was my turn to swallow. "You'd like to..."

"Fuck them."

"Umm. Okay."

His eyes flickered to my neck, and he pointed at it. "I love your collarbone. It's so delicate and pretty. The skin around it is so perfect and smooth."

"Thank you."

"I'm gonna come on it."

"Pardon?"

"All over your neck. After I fuck those gorgeous tits."

I squirmed in my chair. "And when is this happening?"

His eyes rose and locked with mine. They gleamed with wickedness. "Whenever I want."

Maybe it should have upset me that the guy I'd just started dating had just told me at breakfast that he planned to have sex with my breasts and finish all over my neck *whenever he wanted*, but damn...I was game.

I jumped when Rush abruptly pushed his chair back from the table. He walked to where I sat and leaned down to kiss my lips. "Put your shirt back on. I'm trying to be good." He scooped it up from the floor and held it out to me.

I pouted.

"Titty fucking requires at least another date or two." He turned and started to walk out of the kitchen.

"Where are you going? You didn't finish your breakfast."

"Use your imagination, Gia. I'll certainly be using mine."

———

Rush drove me home. Even though I wasn't ready to leave him yet, I really needed to write all day before working tonight. He idled out front instead of parking. "You're on tonight, right?"

I nodded. "Six o'clock."

"How about we do something tomorrow?"

"I'm working brunch starting at eleven."

"I know the boss. I'm sure he'll give you the day off."

I smiled. "Okay! What do you want to do?"

"I was thinking of going in to see my mother. She wants me to meet some asshole she's seeing, and you wanted to see her artwork anyway."

My brows drew together. "She's dating an asshole? How do you know if you haven't met him?"

Rush deadpanned. "He's dating my mother."

I laughed. "And he's automatically an asshole just because he's dating your mother?"

"He starts out as an asshole and has to earn his way out."

I leaned over and brushed my lips with his. "You're lucky I find the protective part of you adorable, because some people really might think you're the one who's the asshole."

"Go write, Shakespeare."

I rubbed my nose back and forth against his. "Maybe I'll write a scene where the hero goes down on the heroine since I have such a nice memory to borrow from."

Rush groaned. "Get out of my car before I have to take another shower."

I chuckled and opened the car door. "Later, boss."

CHAPTER 16

Rush

I should've jerked off a second time this morning.
Considering it was the first time in my life that I was officially *dating* someone, you'd think I wouldn't have to take matters into my own damn hands. Who knew *dating* meant *stroking* multiple times a day.

I glanced over at Gia sitting in the passenger seat. She had on a royal blue silky shorts romper thing with the shoulders cut out. It made her legs look like a mile of smooth skin. I wanted to come on all of that, too.

I raked my fingers through my hair. What the fuck is wrong with me when it comes to this girl? She's sweet and clean, and I want to hear her talk dirty and soil her up. Last night, I tried so hard to keep shit professional at the restaurant. But when she bent over to pick up a stack of menus that fell from the storage room across from my office, I couldn't help myself. I locked the door and sucked on those gorgeous tits until I got her to say she couldn't wait to feel my cock sliding between them. And now, even on the way to my mother's house, I was barely holding my shit together.

Gia kicked off her sandals and put her bare feet up on my dash. "So is the house your mom lives in the same place that you grew up?"

"One and the same. She's been there for thirty-five years."

"That means I'll get to see where you slept as a teenager?"

"Yep."

"I bet you were a handful as a teen. Bringing girls back to your room and what not." She scrunched up her nose. "On second thought...I might not want to go in that room."

"Come on. We can pretend we're fourteen again, and I'll feel you up while sucking your face and pressing a lead pipe into your hip bone."

She laughed. "Fourteen? Is that when you started feeling up girls?"

From her reaction, I figured it best to not tell her it was more like twelve. "Somewhere around there."

"That's young."

"How old were you the first time you got felt up?"

"Eighteen."

My eyes flashed from the road to her to see if she was kidding. She wasn't.

"Eighteen is a little old to go to first base, isn't it?"

She shrugged. "I guess."

"Boys must have been hounding you growing up. I'm guessing the late start had nothing to do with lack of opportunity."

"No. I was asked out a lot. I just..."

I side glanced over at her. "You just what?"

"I don't know. In hindsight, I think I might not have wanted to let my dad down. My mother had acted irresponsibly by having me and taking off. He put so much into raising me. I just didn't want to disappoint him."

All of the girls, and most of the women I spent time with as an adult, had the opposite goal in life. They wanted to piss of their fathers. I'd always kept away from the daddy's girls, telling myself they were prudes. But suddenly I wondered if I had kept away from those girls because I didn't think I could live up to the standards they had. Gia definitely had high expectations and that scared the crap out of me.

"I saw the way your father looks at you, the way you two interact, I don't think it's possible for you to disappoint him."

She smiled. "Anyway, to get back to our conversation. I never had a boy feel me up in his bedroom. But I did let Robbie Kravit put his hand under my sweater in the back row of the movies when we were seniors in high school."

"Is it fucked up that I have the urge to punch Robbie right now?"

She giggled. "Well, now you know how I felt over the last month...women stopping into the restaurant to proposition you while wearing little leather skirts."

I hadn't thought about that. "I didn't invite any of them."

She looked out the window, quiet for a minute and then said, "Can I ask you something?"

"When a woman *asks* if they can ask you something, it's usually not something I want to answer."

She laughed. "Were you with any women since we met?"

"No." I'd almost gone there the night she'd jumped into that fight. But honestly, I had forced myself to reach out to another woman just so I could stop thinking about Gia, and I'm doubtful if I would've even gone through with it if I'd shown up. "I wanted to be with someone because I thought it might stop me from obsessing over you, but I never actually did it."

She nodded and said nothing. Which made me fucking paranoid. *Does she have something to confess?*

"Were you with anyone?"

"No. I've only been with one other person in the last year. And like I told you, that was a total mistake. I got lonely and fell for the nice guy routine because I missed feeling a connection with a man. But I realized after he left me with the wrong number that sex doesn't satisfy the connection I missed."

I shook my head. "Now I want to beat the crap out of the asshole who played you, too. For a variety of reasons. The first being that he got to be inside you and I haven't."

Gia rested her hand high on my thigh, and I almost swerved out of my lane. "We can fix that you know?" she said. "I'm not the one making us take it slow. We just passed a Holiday Inn at the last exit."

I groaned. "You're going to be the death of me, woman."

"Hi!" My mother opened the front door and engulfed Gia in a big hug before even acknowledging me. "I'm so glad you could make it."

The two of them started complimenting each other on shit immediately.

"I love your necklace."

"Blue is your color!"

"Did you change your hair?"

I rolled my eyes. "What the hell am I? Chopped liver?"

My mother stuck out her bottom lip. "*Awww.* Does my little boy feel neglected? Come here. Give your mamma a hug."

Well, now it just feels forced. But I didn't give a crap because my mother's *the shit.* I squeezed her tight, and it felt freaking awesome.

When she pulled back, she looked between Gia and me with the most excited face I've ever seen on her. She clapped her hands a few times, barely able to contain her enthusiasm. "Come in. Come in."

The house I grew up in was small, a typical Cape Cod-style starter home that packed many of the middle-class neighborhoods on Long Island. But my mother kept it filled with bright colors and paintings, so it always felt bigger than most of my friends' homes for some reason. The best thing that came out of my grandfather leaving me the inheritance was that I was able to pay it off for her a few years ago.

"Wow. I love this place." Gia looked around wide-eyed.

"I'm a bit of a wannabe decorator. I change the colors and move the furniture around all the time. When Heathcliff was little, he'd leave for school in the morning and the walls would be tan and couches red and he'd come home and we'd have blue walls and I'd have a staple gun out reupholstering the couches."

Gia smirked at me. "*Heathcliff.* That sounds so funny to me, even though I know it's his name."

"Some of my family call him, Heath. But that never felt right to me."

"Wasn't he named after someone?"

Mom nodded. "My father. He was a good man. But Heathcliff never got the chance to meet him. He died when I was pregnant."

"I'm sorry."

"Thank you. He actually reminds me a lot of my dad. Tough guy, a little rough around the edges, but fiercely loyal and protective."

Gia smiled. "I've definitely noticed the protective side."

"I bet you have. Come on, let me show you my studio before Jeff gets here to take us to his gallery."

"You two go ahead," I said. "I'll meet you there in a few minutes. I'm gonna go out back for a quick smoke."

The two women turned to me and frowned in unison.

"I wish you'd give that up, sweetheart," Mom said.

"Me, too," Gia tacked on.

I looked between the two of them and growled. "Just what I need. Two of you up my ass."

Jeff was nothing like I expected.

He looked more like a grandfather than someone my mother should be dating. Although, I suppose, technically, my mother is old enough to be a grandmother, too. I just never saw her as old because she didn't act it and looked so young.

Jeff had gray hair, tanned skin with deep-set wrinkles, and had on a pair of loafers. I'd never even known she dated, much less got a look at a guy she spent time with, yet I expected him to look more like a rocker than a guy who *sits* in a damn rocker.

"You're awfully quiet," Gia walked up next to me as I pretended to study a painting in Jeff's gallery. It looked like a bunch of ink splats to me, but the price tag was seven grand.

I pointed to the splat. "Would you pay seven grand for that?"

She chuckled. "I don't have seven grand in my bank account. But if I did, I wouldn't be wasting it on that."

"What would you be spending it on?"

"September."

"September?"

She sighed. "Yeah. The house we rent is twenty thousand a month in the summer months, but drops to a fraction of that in September. I just realized I only have six weeks left out there." Our eyes caught. "I'm not ready for it to be over yet."

Yeah. She wouldn't be leaving if I had anything to do with it. I covered my nut for that rental with the spring and summer income. But it was too soon to ask her to stay and tell her I'd foot the bill.

She bumped her shoulder to me. "So...what do you think of your mom's boyfriend?"

"I think he's old as fuck."

She laughed. "Melody said he's only four years older than her."

"He looks forty older."

"Who cares? He seems like a nice guy, and they look happy together."

I glanced over to the other side of the gallery. Jeff and my mother stood in front of a painting and he was telling her something while pointing at the art. Her head bent back in laughter, and my heart squeezed. "Yeah, they do look happy."

"You know..." Gia said, "...people might look at *us* and think we make an odd couple, too. You're all tatted and have that dark and dangerous thing going on. I look like a plain Jane standing next to you."

My eyes raked up and down her. "You're definitely no plain Jane. Maybe a sexy librarian guys fantasize about bending over in between the stacks, but no plain Jane, sweetheart."

She leaned to me. "I wouldn't mind if *you* bent me over in the stacks. In fact, I think that might be kinda hot."

My cock twitched. *Down boy.*

"Oh yeah? How about the bathroom of an art gallery while my mother and her boyfriend are in the next room? Nothing says getting to know your son's girlfriend like listening to her moan while your son rams his cock into her."

Gia jabbed my ribs with her elbow. "Crass."

"You love it. I bet your panties are wet."

She surprised me by leaning up and kissing my cheek before whispering in my ear, "They *are* wet actually. But it's not from hearing you say that you want to ram anything. They're soaked from hearing you refer to me as *your girlfriend* without any hesitation. Total turn on."

I wrapped a hand around her waist and pulled her flush against me. "Oh yeah?"

She nodded with an ear-to-ear smile.

"Come on, *girlfriend*. Let's get this show on the road and have dinner with my mom and grandpa so I can get you back home and get to second base after our second date."

She arched a brow. "Second base? What the hell is second base if you think going down on me is first?"

———

"How's the book coming along, Gia?" my mom asked over dinner.

"It's moving along a little better now. Each day the words are coming a little faster, and the characters are really taking on more of their personalities."

"That's great. I often find it hardest to start a painting, but once I get going, I get into a groove and finish pretty fast."

"I hope that's the case for me. I have a looming deadline."

Mom pointed to me. "My son, on the other hand, can start a painting faster than anyone I've ever met. Yet he never finishes any of them."

Gia's head whipped to me. "You paint?"

I shrugged. "I used to. But haven't painted in years. Found I was better at finishing a piece on a person's skin than I was on canvas though."

"I don't know why I never put two and two together. Your mom is an artist and you used to do tattoos. Of course you must be a talented painter. Do you have any of your old artwork?"

"In a closet somewhere."

"I'd love to see them."

Mom looked between us. "Umm. Rush's art is a little different than mine."

"How so?"

I glanced over at Mom. "I don't paint landscapes."

"Well. Now you have me curious."

"Jeff paints as well," Mom said.

"Not much anymore," Jeff added. "I bought the gallery fifteen years ago as my retirement from painting. But every once in a while, I still get inspired and sit down in front of the old canvas. Though these days, I'm a bit rusty."

"Jeff's being modest." Mom gushed. Something I only ever saw her do when she spoke about me. "He's an amazing painter. One of his paintings was on exhibit at the gallery today."

"Which one?" I asked.

"It was called Ink Splatter."

My eyes jumped to Gia's, and we both lifted our drinks to our mouths in an attempt to hide our smirks.

After dinner and coffee, which was a fuck of a lot less painful to share with the guy my mother is dating than I thought it would be, we headed out to the parking lot. Mom and Gia spent a few minutes talking, and Mom promised she would come out for a long weekend before the end of the summer.

Jeff looked me in the eye and gave a firm handshake. "Your mother is a special woman. Your opinion means the world to her. I'd like to get to know you better. Maybe I could come out for a round of golf one weekend."

"Sure. I'm not that great at golf though. I basically whack the ball as far as I can to try and reach the longest distance."

Jeff smiled. "Good. I suck at it, too. Driving range for an hour, longest drive doesn't have to pay for the beers afterward?"

"Now you're talking." Maybe Grandpa wasn't so bad after all.

The ride home felt like it took forever because I couldn't wait to get my hands on Gia alone. I still didn't think we should seal the deal, but there was no fucking way we were calling it a night without fooling around at least.

I pulled off the expressway and into our neighborhood. "You need anything from your place?"

Her lips slid into an adorable smirk. "That's a bit presumptuous of you, isn't it? You're assuming I'm coming home with you and staying the night?"

"You bet your ass I am. I've been a perfect gentleman all night. That shit stays at the door when we get to my house. I'm going to do filthy things to your body, and you're gonna love it."

She swallowed. "Jesus, Rush."

"I prefer to be called God, as in *Oh God. Oh God.*"

"You're such a jerk."

"True. But do you need anything from your house because I need to make a left at the light if you do."

"No. I'm good."

I side glanced at her. "No pills or anything?"

"Pills?" She was confused what I meant at first, but then it hit her. "Oh! No. I'm not on the pill anymore. I stopped taking them over a year ago since I wasn't...you know, active anymore. But I guess I should get back on them."

Another reason to take things slow. The last thing I needed was to fuck this girl's life up just as she's getting started by knocking her up. And I was pretty certain that when I finally got inside of her, I was gonna shoot such a big load that I'd fill up a condom and that shit would spill over into her.

"If you don't mind taking them, it would be safer that way."

"No, I don't mind. Plus, then we can..."

"Fuck bareback?"

She blushed. "I was gonna say make love without having to stop and put on a condom. But yeah."

My cock swelled at the thought of being inside her bare. I stepped on the gas to get the rest of the way home and practically ran us to the front door. Tossing my keys on the table inside, I said, "Make yourself comfortable. I need to take a quick shower."

She grabbed my hand before I could run off. "Want company?"

I groaned. "You're killing me."

CHAPTER 17

Gia

My nerves started to get the best of me when I heard the shower water turn off. I'd stripped out of all my clothes, rubbed oil all over my breasts, and perched myself on the corner of the bed while I waited for Rush. This would be my first experience having a man slide himself in and out of my cleavage, and I wasn't quite sure what position might work best. Something told me that Rush knew exactly how he'd like it to go down since he seemed to have fantasized about doing it to me before.

He emerged from the bathroom with a towel wrapped around his waist and looking down as he used another one to dry his hair. He froze when he glanced up and saw me. The heat in his eyes pushed out the nervousness that I felt. Rush had a way of making me feel beautiful and desired, without saying a single word.

I reached up and cupped my breasts, pushing them together. "I borrowed some of the oil that I found in your nightstand."

He stared at me for long time. I got the feeling that he was trying to reign himself in. My eyes dropped to the bulge growing in his towel. It *definitely* wasn't working. Unconsciously, I licked my lips, and when I looked up I saw he was watching me.

I nearly stopped breathing when he reached to the knot in his towel and it dropped to the floor.

Jesus.

It was long.

It was thick.

And it was gloriously hard.

The air in the room crackled as we stared at each other.

His voice was gruff. "Get in the center of the bed. Lie on your back."

Once I was settled, he walked over to the edge of the bed and looked down at me as he fisted his cock. "I just came so hard in the shower imagining this."

My entire body was on fire. I was more turned on just thinking about what I was about to experience than I'd ever been during any actual sexual act. Rush lifted a knee to climb onto the bed and then straddled me. I squeezed my breasts together in offering. Locking eyes, he dipped his hips down and guided his cock between my breasts.

His eyes closed as he steadied himself for a few seconds. Then he began to pump fast and furious. I squeezed as hard as I could as he slid his thick length in and out, over and over.

"*Fuck. Fuck.* Your tits feel so good. I'm gonna come all over you. The silky skin on your neck...your beautiful collarbone. I want to paint your entire body with my cum...mark it as mine."

I swallowed. *Jesus Christ.* I loved the way he seemed so possessive of me, as if he couldn't help himself and wanted to dominate my body in an almost animalistic way.

He opened his eyes and stared down. "*Fuck*...so beautiful. So, so perfect."

Watching his orgasm take hold was one of the most magnificent things I'd ever witnessed. The tension in his face coiled as the muscles in his abs went rigid. With a groan of my name that was so sexy it had my own body close to its own release, he let go—exactly how he'd said he'd wanted to—all over my neck.

———

The protectiveness in Rush extended to after care. He cleaned me up with a warm towel, and then returned the favor by going down on me again. Unlike last time though, I didn't pass out from exhaustion right after. While Rush had fallen asleep, I remained awake. My thoughts wandered from obsessing over getting my heart broken to fantasizing about what actual sex would be like with him. The latter led me to think about our conversation earlier and my monthly cycle, when I could start back on the pill.

Wasn't I due for my period?

Would that ruin it for me if he wanted to have sex this week? It was at that moment in the middle of the night, lying in Rush's bed, I realized I couldn't *remember* the last time I'd had a normal cycle. Last month was so light and spotty, but I still assumed it was my period.

And now I'm late.

But how late?

Panic set in.

It couldn't have been that much more than a month ago.

Was it?

Suddenly, I started to *really* panic. I normally marked down the first day of my cycle on my phone calendar. *I needed to know.* I needed to check my phone right now to see when the last time I had marked it down was.

Rush was still out like a light as I moved his arm off of me and slipped past him, making my way over to my purse on the floor.

Taking out my phone, I went straight to the calendar. I scrolled back through the days to check the last time I'd made a note about my period.

Passing over the last month and realizing there was no note entered, I started to feel my heart beating faster. It wasn't until my finger stopped on the date of the last entry that I really started to freak out. The last time I had gotten a normal period was over *two months ago.*

It wouldn't have been so concerning were it not for the fact that I'd had sex with a man prior to that time—my one-night stand from The Heights.

———

The following morning, I tried my best to remain calm for the remainder of my time with Rush. There was no sense in freaking out or jumping to conclusions without a concrete answer.

Rush dropped me off at my house and left me alone to allegedly write.

But there was no writing happening. I must have stared at the wall in my room for several hours.

My eyes wandered over to the sunset painting that Rush's mom had given me. It was an image that once brought me so much joy but that now made me feel pure sadness, a reminder of all of the things I could be missing out on—an entire life of possibilities that might never be.

I'd be seeing Rush tonight again and didn't know how I was going to face him unless I knew for certain. Yet, I just couldn't get myself to go to the store and buy a pregnancy test.

How could I have put myself in a position where this was even a remote possibility? I'd done my best all my life to make sound decisions. That night with Harlan was one of the few times I had truly screwed up. I mean, I didn't even know his last name or if his name was really Harlan. I couldn't contact him if I wanted to. I had been feeling vulnerable and depressed about my career when I met him, and he'd provided a distraction, charmed the pants off of me—literally. But it was a huge mistake. To think that one mistake in judgment could possibly mean my ending up with a lifetime of responsibility was unfathomable.

I could barely take care of myself; I wasn't ready to be a single mother.

It would break my dad's heart.

And that scenario would surely be the end of Rush and me. He was hesitant to commit to a relationship as it was, let alone get involved with a girl carrying another man's child—a man who'd disappeared.

Placing my head in my hands, I thought back to last night, how amazing it felt to be with Rush. I was falling so hard for him. I knew he was taking it physically slower with me than he was used to. And that made my need for him even stronger. I wanted him so badly in every way. Now, I might never get to have any part of him. Unless this result was negative, I might never experience what it would be like to *truly* be with Rush.

I needed to know.

I was seriously afraid that I'd have a heart attack if it were positive. Unsure if I could handle taking the test alone, I pondered whether I could trust Riley with this secret.

If it turned out she was in her room, I'd tell her. If she wasn't, that would be my sign from above to keep this to myself.

Riley was sitting in front of her vanity, curling waves into the front of her hair when I interrupted.

She could immediately tell something was wrong from the look on my face as I stood in her doorway.

She put down her curling iron. "Did something happen?"

My tone was firm. "Riley, you need to promise me you won't say anything to anyone."

"What the...did Rush do something?"

"No, no. Rush is...amazing. This doesn't have anything to do with him." Sitting down on her bed, I got right to the point. "Do you remember the one-night stand I had with that guy from The Heights?"

"The one who gave you the wrong number. Yeah."

"Well, I'm scared he might have left me with more than just a wrong number."

Her eyes widened. "Do you have a disease?"

I shook my head. "No. At least, I hope not."

"What, then?"

"I had a spotty period last month, and I'm late now."

She covered her mouth. "Oh my God."

My voice was trembling. "I'm scared, Riley. Really scared."

"Does Rush know?"

"Of course not. I can't even imagine how he'd react. This would completely blindside him. We've really gotten close, to the point where I think I…" I couldn't say the words, even though I felt them deep inside my heart.

She read my mind. "You're falling in love with him."

Yes.

Tears started to stream down my cheeks as I nodded in silence. I was totally losing it now.

"Come here." Riley moved over to the bed and embraced me.

"I have to find out, but I'm scared."

She took a deep breath in then blew it out slowly. "Okay, tell you what. You stay here. Try not to panic. I'll go to the store and buy a test. Ironically, I have to run and get condoms for my date tonight."

I sniffled. "Alright."

"It's going to be interesting when the cashier rings me up for condoms *and* a pregnancy test." She grinned.

"Staring at the box isn't going to make this situation go away. There's only one way to know," she said.

"I know."

Forcing myself up off the bed, I ventured into the bathroom and numbly opened the package, following the directions and peeing on the stick.

With my heart pounding, I walked back out to the bedroom where Riley was waiting and exhaled.

I sat down on the bed and she joined me.

Riley rubbed my back. "Just breathe, Gia."

"Five minutes." I sighed.

My phone chimed, nearly scaring the crap out of me because my nerves were so sensitized.

When I reached for it, I realized it was a text from Rush.

Rush: Remember that shower you wanted to take with me last night...but I wouldn't let you? Yeah, I think it might have to be on tonight. I can't stop thinking about lathering up those delicious tits but not before I slide between them again. Okay with you?

That message would have normally made me so excited about tonight. Instead, an unimaginable pain filled me. I already felt like I'd lost him somehow. It was hard to imagine not having Rush around anymore. He'd consumed every part of my life from the moment I first met him.

I guess I should write back.

Gia: I miss you already.

He had no idea that there was deeper meaning in that statement. I already missed what I knew I could potentially be losing in a matter of minutes.

It was past the time to look at the test now. The results would be there. I just couldn't get myself to go back in the bathroom.

"You want me to check it?" she asked.

Swallowing nervously, I rubbed my palms on my thighs. "Yeah. Please."

Riley crossed the hall and entered the bathroom. It felt like the longest thirty seconds of my life.

When she came back, her face was flush. She looked sullen.

She didn't even have to say anything.

I knew.

My phone chimed.

Rush: You've fucked me up, Gia. I'm crazy for you.

His words were like a knife to the heart and couldn't have come at a worse possible time.

Feeling numb, I closed my eyes, and Riley pulled me into a side hug. Leaning my head on her shoulder, I knew I was going to have to tell him. But I needed just one more night.

One more night where it was just Rush and me.

One more night before I inevitably lost him.

CHAPTER 18

Rush

Gia insisted that we stay in tonight. She said she wasn't feeling well and just wanted to spend time with me at my place.

I wasn't gonna argue with that. After a long day of making the rounds at several different properties and getting into it with this one contractor, there was nothing I wanted more than to just chill with my girl.

Whoa.

My girl.

Fuck. Did I just think that?

I did.

Gia was *my* girl.

What was happening to me that I actually *loved* the thought of being tied down? Tied up. Whatever. Fact is, I'd never wanted to be attached until she came along and taught me that there was a first time for everything.

Well, damn.

I couldn't remember the last time I'd had a girlfriend. It was probably in high school, but even then, my relationships were short-lived. I used to think

I didn't want it. But now, I realize it was just that the right person hadn't come along.

Gia had insisted on driving herself to my place. That was fine with me because it gave me extra time to make something for us to eat. Cooking wasn't my forte, but I was one hell of a griller. I could marinate the fuck out of some vegetables and meat, throw it all on skewers and slap them on the grill. I made pilaf in the rice cooker and threw some garlic bread in the oven. Earlier I'd stopped at the liquor store to pick up Gia's favorite Moscato. That definitely elevated my pussy-whipped status up by a notch.

When she knocked on the door, I put my beer down and went to let her in.

Her shoulders were rising and falling as she stood in the doorway. She looked anxious. She was wearing a red strapless dress, and her flushed skin looked like it was trying to compete with the color of her outfit.

Gia lifted her hand. "Hey."

I pulled her into a hug, and that turned into me lifting her up in the air as she wrapped her legs around me. I kissed her so hard, sucking all the clear gloss off her lips.

When I put her down, I couldn't help noticing how good her tits looked.

They looked huge, like they wanted to spill out of that dress.

"I missed you today," I said.

Pussy. Whipped.

"I missed you, too."

When I finally pried my eyes away from her breasts and looked up at her face, I noticed that it seemed like her eyes were watery.

My brows furrowed. "Are you...crying?"

She sniffled. "I don't know what's wrong with me. I just got emotional all of a sudden. I'm sorry. That happens to me sometimes. It's random. I'm fine." She wiped her eyes. "Really happy, actually. I promise."

I didn't know what to make of that. I just knew I needed to taste her lips again. Caressing her cheek, I brought her mouth to mine.

Gia took a deep breath in. "Something smells really delicious."

"I grilled us up some dinner. Thought it was about time you sampled my meat." I winked.

When she didn't respond to that with laughter—in fact, when she didn't respond at all—I knew something was still preoccupying her. It was unlike Gia not to come back with something.

Placing my hand around her waist and inching her closer to me, I said, "You sure you're okay?"

"Yes." She smiled.

We ended up eating dinner on the deck. We both devoured the steak tips with mushrooms, peppers, onions, and zucchini. Gia said she didn't feel like any of the wine, which was odd. So, I tried to make her something else. Even trying to get her to say a dirty word in exchange for a Cosmo didn't work.

We watched the sun setting as I sipped my own wine while she drank water. Hanging out on my deck like this was becoming our thing.

After dinner, Gia sat in between my legs as we stared out at the dark ocean.

Her hair was blowing in the breeze when she suddenly said, "I want to learn everything about you, Rush. I don't want to miss anything there is to know."

"We have plenty of time for that, don't we?"

She turned around momentarily when she said, "No one knows how much time we ever have."

I squeezed her. "Okay, Miss Morbid. What do you want to know? I'll tell you. Anything at all. Shoot."

"What's your favorite color?"

"Black."

"No surprise there. It suits you." She chuckled. "Um...where do you see yourself in ten years?"

"That's a bit of a jump..."

"I know. I'm just asking questions as they pop into my head."

I thought about her question then said, "I honestly don't know, Gia. I know the typical answer that most people would give is...married with kids and a dog or some shit. But I'm not most people. That was never how I saw my life. But I'm realizing lately that what I thought I wanted and what I actually want might be different. I don't have a clear grasp on what ten years from now or even tomorrow looks like." I spoke against the back of her neck. "I hope you'll just wing this with me."

She turned around and answered me silently with a kiss.

Then she blurted out, "How many women have you been with?"

I should've seen this coming at some point.

"Why do you even want to know that?"

"Morbid curiosity, I guess."

I sighed. "I honestly don't know. I never counted." I wanted to give her something, so I estimated. "If I had to guess? Maybe fifty."

"Wow. Ok."

"Wow?" I mimicked. "Tell me what you're thinking."

"I honestly didn't know what to expect there. I thought maybe it could even be more than that."

I didn't really know if I wanted to know the answer, but I asked anyway. "How many men have you slept with?"

"Five," she answered without hesitation.

I suddenly wanted to kill five men I'd never met.

"That's not that bad," I said.

"It is what it is, right?"

"Yeah," I said, still a little jealous, which was fucked-up.

Gia hesitated before she asked. "Have you ever been in love?"

She was definitely hitting me with all the big questions tonight.

There was only one relationship in my life that ever came close to that. Since we seemed to be opening up tonight, I decided to tell her a story.

"The closest I ever came was with a girl named Beth. She was my best friend growing up. Her father was actually like the closest thing I had to a dad. His name is Pat. He was super cool and I used to go to him for advice about...you know, dude stuff. Shaving and shit. Anyway, they lived only a few doors down from us."

"What did she look like?"

"She had brown hair, not as dark as yours, though. She was pretty. She actually wore glasses like you sometimes. We were close. But I never looked at her in a sexual way—until we were about seventeen."

She swallowed. "Then what happened?"

"I wish I knew what the turning point was. I guess it was just teenage hormones doing their thing. I didn't really think anything like that would ever happen with her. I never wanted to go there. Anyway, one night...it did...we ended up having sex, and it really put a strain on our relationship."

Gia sighed. "Wow."

"There was no way I was ready for anything serious. She wanted more after that, and I just couldn't commit to anything that young. But I really *did* care about her. And I always regretted hurting her. We were kids. And she was practically family. Things were really never the same after that happened."

"Where is she today?"

"After we graduated from high school, her father ended up getting a job out in Arizona. When her parents and brother moved out there, she followed them even though she was old enough to stay out here on her own if she really wanted to. I think if I'd begged her to stay, she would have. But like I said, I wasn't ready for that. So, she moved."

"Do you ever talk to her anymore?"

"We've kept in touch. She's actually married now with a kid. So, everything worked out the way it was supposed to."

"I bet she still fantasizes about you." She smiled.

I pulled her into me. "Oh yeah? What makes you think that?"

"Because I couldn't imagine having sex with you and having to go back to being just friends."

"Well, you won't have to worry about that. I have no interest in *only* being friends with you ever again. Because my intentions are completely impure when it comes to you, and I don't anticipate that ever changing." I laughed.

She ran her fingers through my hair then posed another question, one that threw me for a loop a little. "Do you believe in God?"

My feelings on that were complex. I did my best to offer an explanation of how I saw things when it came to spirituality.

"Yes. I do. Well, at least, I believe there's something powerful that watches over all of us. But the only thing that's certain to me is that we weren't meant to know everything. Anyone who claims to understand exactly how this complex universe works is a fucking liar. Or they're believing what they want to. We all just have to do our best with what knowledge we have and have a little bit of blind faith. We get signs every day that tell us whether we're on the right path. People and opportunities are placed before us. You know that feeling you get when something feels truly right in life? Like all the stars finally aligned? That trust you feel that the universe has sent you exactly what you need—even if you didn't realize you needed it?

"Yes."

"Well, that to me is God."

She stayed quiet, soaking in my answer. For some reason, since we were being open, I had the urge to share something with her that I hadn't shared with anyone other than my mother.

I nudged her up. "Can I show you something?"

"Yeah."

With our hands locked together, I led her to a spare room inside at the back of my house. It was where I housed my own artwork along with all of my tattoo equipment that I never parted with. I still dabbled in design, mainly word of mouth stuff, friends who wanted new ink.

She walked around, gazing at the paintings on the wall.

"I made these."

"These...are yours?"

I nodded.

It wasn't that I was ashamed of what I'd created, but these weren't the type of images you flaunted in the middle of your living room. From the time I was a teenager, I'd had an obsession with painting beautiful women...but not just any women—sexy, sensual women with wings. I don't know if you could consider them fantasy angels or fairies. But they all had a few things in common, long hair, sexy, voluptuous bodies, piercing eyes—and wings. Some were naked. Others were clothed. I could totally see how the average woman might find these images creepy, but I suspected that Gia wouldn't. I knew she was open-minded and would find the artistic value in them.

"I don't even know why I'm showing you these," I said. "You seemed so interested in my mother's art. Obviously, these are a lot different than...sunsets."

"Yeah, they are. They're absolutely stunning— breathtaking." She stopped in front of one of the darker images, a demonic-looking girl with black wings and horns. "What made you decide to start making these?"

Shrugging, I said, "I wish I knew. I just find them to be beautiful and mysterious. I haven't actually created one in a few years, though. These are all pretty old. And you'll notice, each one is slightly unfinished. It's like I would get hung up on making it perfect then move on to the next one out of frustration."

She smiled. "I almost feel jealous of them. That's how beautiful they are. Is that strange?"

Well, I'd take that as a compliment.

I chuckled. "They don't compare to you. They're fantasy. All the things that make them beautiful...the strength they seem to convey... that's all brought to life whenever I look at you, whenever I'm with you."

Gia looked like she was trying to fend off tears again. Was it something I said?

She walked over to where I kept all of my ink supplies.

"Oh my God. Is this where you tattoo people?"

"I rented space in a shop back when I was doing it for a living. But I took all my stuff with me. So, I have a little setup here."

In the corner of the room, I had a table along with various pieces of equipment: a steam pressure autoclave, needle bar setups, and several sealed containers to keep things sterile.

"Can I ask you something?" she said.

"Shoot."

"Would you do anything for me?" She reached up and wrapped her arms around my neck.

Leaning down, I tasted her lips then said, "Pretty sure I would, yeah. Unless you said you wanted me to let you fuck another dude while I watched. That's a hard limit. I don't share."

"Well, then this request will seem like nothing compared to that."

"What is it?"

"Will you draw something small on my body tonight? I want you to choose where it goes and what it is. Not a permanent tattoo or anything—just your artwork on my body. I want something created by you just for me."

I expelled a breath. She knew how I felt about actually tattooing her, that I'd refused to do it. She'd asked me to before, and I'd said no. It wasn't that I didn't want to put my mark on her. I just didn't want her to regret altering her perfect body if she wasn't absolutely sure about it. So, this seemed harmless.

"You really want me to draw on your skin?"

"I really want you to. Yes...please."

The urgency in her request was odd, but at the same time, the prospect of getting to mark her—albeit temporarily—with something of my choice excited me.

"You're a pain in the ass," I teased.

Her face brightened as she realized I was giving in to her request.

"Thank you!" She beamed.

"Go lie on the table, but first, take off your clothes. Take off everything."

She did as I said and made her way over to the table I had set up.

She was stark naked. "How do you want me?"

"There are so many ways I could answer that question." My dick stiffened to full mast as I said, "Lie on your stomach first."

Gia did as I said, and suddenly, I was staring at her beautiful ass face-up on the table. I softly kissed her back, lowering my mouth slowly down to her butt cheeks.

I knew exactly where I wanted to put my mark on her but was too worked up to even start. I needed to make her squirm first.

Taking my finger to my mouth, I licked it before slipping it between her legs and into her pussy. She flinched at the contact. I added my index finger and pushed deeper into her. With my thumb firmly placed on her ass, I moved my two fingers in an out of her hole as she wriggled under my hand. I was so tempted to replace my fingers with my cock. But before I could even really consider that, her hands gripped the table as she moved her ass in sync with the motion of my fingers. Then, I could feel her pulsating around my hand as she came.

It was a beautiful sight as she panted with her face down on the table.

As she came down from her orgasm, I rubbed my calloused palm over the soft skin of her ass.

"You ready?"

Out of breath, she rolled over onto her back, her beautiful tits bouncing. "I hope you don't give all your clients orgasms before working on them."

"Only you, baby." I leaned down one last time to take her nipple into my mouth. I was hard as fuck, but I'd promised her some ink. "Get on your stomach again."

I knew exactly what design I wanted for her and began drawing it onto her lower back just above her ass crack. It had been a long time, but I didn't feel rusty at all. I used a violet-colored pen, just the color I'd choose if this were permanent ink.

It took me about ten minutes.

"Ready to see it?"

"Oh my God. Yes."

I helped Gia down from the table, and she walked her gorgeous, naked body over to a mirror on the wall. She turned her head to look at what I'd drawn on her.

Her eyes focused in on the small pair of wings on the bottom of her back.

"You gave me wings." Her mouth spread into a wide grin. "Now, I'm one of your girls."

I pulled her into me. "No. You're *the* girl. I don't have to imagine anything anymore."

———

Somehow I managed to not lose control as she slept in my bed that night.

We messed around, but we didn't fuck. I knew without a shadow of a doubt that I couldn't wait any longer, though. If she was down, the next night we were together, I was going to have her. I needed to be inside of her.

Gia's car wouldn't start when she tried to leave my place the next morning. I couldn't believe it; that piece of shit had died again after I'd just fixed it. So, I gladly drove her home in my Mustang.

When we got there, I needed to take a leak badly, so I used the small bathroom off the hallway just outside of her bedroom.

As I shook my cock off into the toilet, I looked down at the trash bin and noticed the packaging of a pregnancy test.

Hmm.

There were two sticks in the garbage, too. Being the nosy motherfucker that I am, I lifted them out and noticed two pink lines on each of them.

Someone in this house was pregnant.

But who?

This bathroom was shared by three of the bedrooms. Gia and Riley had their own rooms, and then the other bedroom off of this hall was shared by two dudes.

The stick must have belonged to Riley.

Yeah.

It had to be.

Well, it couldn't be Gia. I knew that. Because she hadn't fucked anyone.

My heart was pounding.

Right? It couldn't be.

She hadn't fucked anyone.

Except for that guy from The Heights.

But she had to have used protection, right?

As the seconds passed, I became more and more paranoid.

"Everything okay in there?" I heard Gia ask.

"Yeah." I shouted through the door.

My mind wandered back to last night. I started thinking more about some of her odd behavior.

All the questions—implying there was no time.

The crying.

The tits. *Holy shit.* Her tits, which looked like they had grown from the last time I'd seen her.

It couldn't be.

No.

No.

No.

The stick was still in my shaking hand as I flexed my fingers, letting it once again fall into the trash.

When I opened the door, Gia was standing there looking like she'd seen a ghost. She was trembling... freaking out.

She'd figured out her fuck-up—that she'd left the tests in the garbage.

Adrenaline shot through me as the words exited my mouth. "Are you pregnant?"

CHAPTER 19

Gia

I thought my heart had broken when I looked at the results of the pregnancy test. But it hadn't. It had cracked, yet continued to beat. I knew this the moment I looked into Rush's eyes—because that was the moment that those cracks gave way and my heart shattered into a million little pieces. I couldn't even respond to him. I just stood there and let the tears stream down my face. The pain in Rush's eyes matched the excruciating ache inside of my chest.

"Fuck!" he screamed.

"*Fuck!*" He tugged fistfuls of his hair with both hands.

"Fuck. Fuck. *Fuuuuucccck.*"

Riley whipped open her bedroom door and ran into the hallway looking like we'd woken her. "What's going on? Is everything okay?"

She took one look at us and knew what had just gone down. Mouthing *I'm sorry*, she turned and slipped back into her bedroom, shutting the door quietly behind her.

My eyes caught with Rush's.

"Say it, Gia." His voice was the type of calm that happened in the eye of the storm. You know there's a big swirl growing and growing that will hit even harder very soon, and you can only brace for it.

"I'm sorry," I whispered. "I don't know how it happened."

"You don't know *how it fucking happened*?"

My tears had been silent, but the bubble burst. Sobs shook my shoulders and weakened my legs as I lowered to the floor.

"Fuck," Rush gritted.

"Fuck."

"Fuck. Fuck. *Fuuuuuucccck*."

Through my blurred vision, I saw him move, and for a few horrible seconds, I thought he was leaving, thought he was going to walk past me sitting on the floor and right out the front door. But then suddenly, I was in the air and in Rush's arms. He scooped me up and carried me into my bedroom. Kicking the door closed behind him, he walked to the bed and gently set me down.

"We used protection. I swear we did. And it was only once. I've only had sex with *one person* in more than a year, *one time* and this happens."

Rush sat next to me and just kept nodding.

"I'm sorry I didn't tell you. I only found out yesterday and...I just couldn't say it out loud yet."

Long minutes went by, and he continued to just sit there and nod. "Say something, please," I whispered while wiping away tears.

He couldn't even look at me. "You said you don't even know the guy's number."

I looked down and shook my head.

"What kind of a piece of shit doesn't even give a woman the right contact information?"

"The kind who doesn't want to be involved in your life after one night."

Rush took a deep breath and let it out. Then he finally turned to face me. *"Jesus Christ.* Have you thought about what you're going to do?"

"I haven't been able to think about anything, Rush. Honestly, I've been so worried about what *you* would think; it hasn't really sunk in yet. I know I can't have an abortion, though. If my Mom had..."

Rush reached over and took my hand. "I know. I get it."

We sat in quiet again. Eventually, I said, "I'm not ready to be a mother. I live in a studio apartment in Queens, and I have a one-book commitment from a publisher with a tiny advance, which they'll probably have to sue me to get back when I don't turn in a manuscript on time. I don't know the first thing about babies, or being a mother, for that matter. I didn't even have a maternal example growing up. But what terrifies me the most is..." I turned to face him and he looked up into my eyes. "...what does this all mean between you and me?"

"Gia..." Rush raked his hand through his hair for what seemed like the tenth time. "I don't have any answers."

I didn't have a right to be mad at his noncommittal response. I'd gotten myself into this predicament, and I wasn't naïve enough to think this didn't change everything. But that didn't mean it wouldn't crush me to feel him pulling away.

Rush's phone chimed, and he pulled it from his pocket. "Shit. The liquor company is at The Heights with my delivery. I'm supposed to be there now to accept it."

"Go." I forced a smile. "Can't run a bar without liquor, and unfortunately my predicament isn't going anywhere in a hurry."

He stood. "Yeah. Alright. I'll...I'll see you later." Rush walked a few steps toward my bedroom door and then came back to where I still sat on the bed. "Get some rest." He kissed the top of my head. Somehow I managed to keep the tears in until he walked out, and I heard his car start out front. Then I let it all out. I cried and cried, until eventually I cried myself to sleep.

———

"What's up, Gia?" Oak lifted his chin when I walked into work early for my shift. I hadn't heard from Rush all day and hoped he'd be here so maybe we could talk again. The initial shock had probably turned into something different by now, and I wondered what he was feeling. His Mustang hadn't been in the parking lot when Riley dropped me off, but my car was. He must've gotten it started somehow.

I went to the office and knocked. After waiting a few minutes, I took a deep breath and cracked the door open. *Empty.* My pulse sped up as I wandered around the main floor of the restaurant looking for him. Every time I thought he might be behind a door—in the kitchen, the supply room, the back—I held my breath as I took a peek. Each time he wasn't there, I was disappointed and relieved at the same time.

On my way upstairs, the phone rang. I'd forgotten to grab it from the office where it normally sat on the charger on Rush's desk overnight. But the sound was coming from the dining area. Someone had left it at the hostess station along with my car keys. I answered the phone and took a reservation for seven o'clock. A barstool that wasn't usually at the hostess station was also set up there, though it wasn't one of the ones from the bar. It was leather, and padded with a nice tall back. After the call, I stayed sitting in it for a few more minutes and practiced some deep breaths before heading to the stairs. The only place left where Rush could be was up on the rooftop bar.

But when I got upstairs, no one was around except for Oak. He was behind the bar changing out a beer keg. I walked over. "Oak? Do you know where Rush is?"

"Haven't seen him since he dropped off your chair and car."

My chair?

"He's not here?"

"Nope." He finished pushing the keg into its tight space and wiped his hands on a towel. "Figured you knew that. He left your car keys and that chair he bought. Said he was taking the night off."

My stomach clenched. "Oh. Okay. Thank you."

I sulked my way back down the stairs and went to dig my phone from my purse. I hadn't checked it since I'd left the house. Maybe Rush had texted to let me know he wouldn't be in tonight. Of course, deep down, I knew from the empty feeling in the pit of my stomach that there'd be no text. But that didn't stop me from checking.

An overwhelming sadness came over me when I confirmed he hadn't sent a text. I tried to tell myself that it didn't mean anything. Rush just needed some time to let everything sink in. Who wouldn't? It hadn't truly sunk in for me yet either.

When Oak came back downstairs, I forced myself to get busy. Work would at least be a distraction. I did my usual pre-opening routine, although I set up my cellphone to vibrate when any new texts came in and then slipped it into my pocket while I went about getting everything ready for the night. Even though it never vibrated, I checked it incessantly anyway.

Oak stopped by the hostess station while I was slipping the paper with the printed daily specials into the plastic menu jackets. "Five minutes to opening, G."

"Okay. Thanks." When he started to walk away, a thought dawned on me. "Oak?"

He turned back. "Hmmm?"

"Where is this chair I'm sitting on supposed to go? You said Rush dropped it off. Does it belong in the office?"

"Nope. He said something about the hostesses needing a place to rest their feet." He winked. "But I'm pretty sure there's only one hostess whose feet Rush gives a crap about."

Despite the sadness I felt from Rush not making contact at all today and taking the night off, which I suspected was to avoid me, I latched on to the fact that he'd taken the time to go out and buy a chair so that I could have a place to rest if I needed it. Not to mention, he'd also fixed my car to make sure I wouldn't walk home. It was crazy to even think about, but Rush would make a really great father with all his protectiveness.

The restaurant stayed busy for the next few hours, so at least I couldn't sit around obsessing too much over my situation. Forced smiles and friendly chitchat were basically most of my job. But by ten o'clock when things slowed down, and I'd practically killed my phone battery from constantly checking for a message that never arrived, I had no more fake smiles to give.

Oak noticed and stopped by. "You okay, G?"

"Yeah. Just a bit tired." It wasn't a lie. I was exhausted, both emotionally and physically.

Oak raised a single eyebrow. "Mmm-hmm. Boss looked *just a bit tired* when he stopped in, too."

"Did he...say anything?"

"If you haven't noticed, Rush is a thinker, not much of a talker."

That comment was awarded my first genuine smile of the evening.

Oak looked over my shoulder into the dining room. "Looks like you only have one table left. They all finished?"

"Yeah. Just sipping their coffee. The waitress left them the bill, but they aren't rushing to pay it so I can run the credit card."

He nodded his head toward the door. "Go home. I'll run the card. Get some rest. While you're at it, call the man and tell him you forgive him for whatever stupid shit he did wrong."

I wished it were that easy. "You sure you don't mind?"

"Go home. Bossman would kick my ass if he knew I didn't send you home when you needed to go."

"Thanks, Oak."

———

I drove home in a fog. It was stupid of me, and in the future, I probably shouldn't put myself at risk like that if I'm not feeling alert enough to drive. It wasn't just me anymore I needed to think about. When I pulled up to my house, I killed the ignition and relaxed back into the driver's seat. For the first time, I put my hand on my stomach. It felt surreal to acknowledge that there was a person growing inside of me.

"Hey. I'm...well, I guess I'm your mom." I rubbed a gentle circle just below my belly button. "I feel like I should have introduced myself by now. But, I only found out you existed yesterday." *God. Has it really only been one day?*

I took a deep breath. "I just wanted you to know that just because you weren't planned, doesn't mean that I'll ever make you feel like you are unwanted. My dad used to say, 'Life is ten percent of what happens to you and ninety percent what you make of it.' And you and me, we're going to make the best of it. Just like my dad and I did."

Finished with my odd little introduction, I pulled my phone from the car charger, tossed the keys into my purse, and got out of the car. As I walked to the front door, I couldn't help but check my text messages again. After all, the fifteen-minute drive home was probably the longest stretch I'd gone without checking all day.

But...nothing was there. *Again.*

Looking down while I wallowed in self-pity, I made it almost to the door when a voice scared the crap out of me. "Gia."

I jumped, and my hand whipped to my chest. Rush was standing in the dark in front of my door. "Holy crap. How long have you been standing there?"

"A while," he said. "I was here waiting when you pulled up. It looked like you needed to take a minute in the car, so I didn't want to walk over."

"Yeah...I..." I looked over my shoulder behind me. Had I been that unaware of my surroundings that I hadn't even seen his car when I pulled up? But I still didn't see it. "Where's your car?"

"I walked here."

"That has to be at least a few miles."

Rush shrugged. "I was drinking earlier, and I needed some time to think anyway. The walk did me good."

Our gazes locked. "Oh."

"You feel up to talking?"

"Of course." I went to step forward to open the front door, and Rush stopped me.

"Would you mind if we sat in the yard? Maybe the lounge chairs to talk?"

"Sure. Can I get you a drink or something?"

Rush shook his head. "No thanks. I'm good."

He stepped aside and put his hand out for me to walk first. While we made our way to the gate leading to the backyard, I wondered why he didn't want to come in. Did he not want to be alone with me in my room? Did he think there would be yelling and he wanted privacy? Could I be overthinking it, and he just wanted to enjoy the nice weather tonight?

In the yard, Rush pulled two lounge chairs together and sat down on the edge of one facing me. I took his lead and sat across from him. The outside security lights had illuminated when we'd walked by, so I caught the first up-close look at him in the light.

Rush looked awful. Like he'd gone on a bender and someone ran over his dog while he watched. His hair definitely had withstood a continuation of this morning's tug-of-war.

He rested his elbows on his knees and hung his head. "How are you feeling?"

"Physically, I'm good. Tired. But good."

"You're going to need more rest. Keep off your feet when you can."

I smiled. "Well, I can do that at work now. Thanks to you."

He nodded. "I did a lot of thinking today."

"Okay..."

"I thought about the things you said that you're worried about: You're not ready. You live in a studio apartment. You don't have a steady job and you don't know how to be a mother."

Wow. He'd really listened. "I didn't mean to unload all of my problems on you. I was just rambling because I'm scared."

"Well, you need to reduce stress now. Not increase it worrying about things. So I want to help."

My hopes rose. "What do you mean?"

"First, the studio apartment in Queens. There's something I haven't mentioned to you about your summer rental."

"What?"

"I own it."

"You *bought* the house?"

"Not today. I meant I'm the owner you rented from, well, my corporation is. This house and two others out here were part of my inheritance from my grandfather. He actually owned a bunch, and he split them up between my brother, my father and me—like he did with a lot of his other businesses."

"Why didn't you say anything?"

Rush chuckled. "I have no fucking idea. I thought it was funny at first, an odd coincidence, and then I just forgot about that you didn't know."

"That's so weird. There are thousands of houses out here, and you *happen* to own the one that I'm renting for the summer? And I *happen* to get a job in your bar?"

"My mother would say someone up there..." He shook his thumb up at the sky. "...wanted us to meet."

I smiled. "I'd have to say I agree with her."

"Anyway. It's not rented after Labor Day. Normally, I just get a couple of straggler rentals for a few weekends here and there in the off-season, not much until next summer. If I calculated correctly, your due date will be the end of the winter. Stay out here. Use the house over the winter rent-free. You can give up your studio apartment in Queens and save some money until next summer comes."

Wow. Totally not what I expected, but it was also a lot more than I could accept from him. "Rush...that's very generous of you, but..."

He raised his hand stopping me. "Let me finish. This solves a lot of your worries, not just the studio apartment one. You want to write—the book you're writing is set in the Hamptons. You said yourself you'd be happy if you could turn it into a series. Well, you'll write that series better by staying out here. And, I pretty much lose my entire staff after Labor Day. The restaurant closes in October, but I keep the bar open year-round. It turns into a bunch of locals who don't drink all the stupid shit that the summer brats out here drink. So I'll teach you how to make a few drinks, and you can stay on as my bartender so that you have steady work."

"Rush...I don't know what to say..."

His hand went up again. "Not done yet."

I smiled, my hopes growing by the minute. "Okay."

"The last thing you're worried about—not ready to be a mother. I can't really help you there, myself. But I have the perfect person who can—my mother raised me alone. I'm sure she would love to come out and spend time with you and teach you mom shit."

"Mom shit..."

"Whatever you need to learn to make yourself feel better."

This morning I'd dropped a bomb on this man, and instead of getting pissed off and running for the hills, he'd spent the day trying to solve all of my problems for me. And he had most of it figured out. It was incredibly generous and thoughtful. But he'd missed the most important part of what I'd said this morning. Or maybe he hadn't...

"Rush. That is the most kind and generous offer that anyone has ever attempted to give me. And I truly appreciate it more than you will ever know. But..." I wasn't sure how to say what I really wanted after he'd just given me so much.

"What?"

"I did say all those things. And I don't want you to think I don't appreciate all that you're offering and how much you thought about things today. But the point of me telling you all of that earlier wasn't so that you can solve my problems. The point was, when I was done telling you how afraid I am of all those things..." I took a deep breath and locked gazes with Rush before getting to the most important part. "I told you I was afraid of all those things and yet what terrifies me the most is...what happens between me and you now."

Rush's eyes told me the answer before he found the words. He looked distraught and sad, mixed with a touch of what I thought might be guilt. With a deep breath, he reached forward and squeezed my knee.

"I'm sorry, Gia. I really am. I just...I'm not ready for a family. I wasn't even sure if I saw a serious relationship in my life at all before I met you. It's why I kept trying to slow us down. You're an amazing woman, and I want to help you however I can. But shit just got real, and now it's not just you I'll fuck up when I eventually...I just...I'm not ready for this."

It felt like a fifty-pound weight had settled onto my chest. It made it hard to breathe. "I understand."

He squeezed my knee again to get my attention. Rush looked as sad as I felt. "Stay in the house. Work the winter at The Heights. Let me help in that way, at least."

The taste of salt in my throat told me I wasn't going to be able to hold back the tears much longer. Rush felt bad enough. He was trying to do the right thing as much as he could. This wasn't his burden to carry. I stood. "It's a lot to think about. But I really appreciate your offer."

"Gia..." He stood. It was torture not being able to reach out and touch him in the moment.

"I gotta go inside. Nature calls."

He looked crestfallen but nodded.

I held my head high as I hurried to the door—hoping, just hoping, that I could disguise my running away as bravery and make it a little bit easier for Rush.

CHAPTER 20

Gia

Morning sickness apparently doesn't always come in the morning.

Tonight's special was pan-fried salmon and garlic parmesan roasted asparagus. I'd always loved the smell of the kitchen at The Heights, until I walked in two nights after my conversation with Rush. I had to literally run to the bathroom where I proceeded to lose the little bit I had eaten during the day.

My head hung over the toilet as I dry heaved. Nothing was left, but apparently my stomach didn't get the message. The bathroom door creaked open then shut.

"You okay?" Rush's voice was low.

I gagged when I opened my mouth to answer.

"What can I do?" From the closeness of his voice, I knew he was standing right on the other side of the stall door.

"Could you maybe get me something to drink? Some caffeine-free Coke?"

"Sure. Be right back." The door opened and closed and a few minutes later, Rush was back inside the ladies' room.

"Do you want me to slip it under the door. Or are you coming out?"

I reached up and unlatched the bolt that kept the door shut but didn't get up from the floor. Rush gently pushed it open. He knelt down next to me with a glass of soda. "Here you go."

I took a few hesitant sips and shook my head. "Thanks. I'm sorry. I didn't see that coming. I just walked into the kitchen, and I guess the smell got to me." After being off yesterday, the first contact I had with this man had to be in a bathroom stall. More proof that he should run the other way.

Rush sat down on the floor next to me. "Don't apologize. If men had to go through the shit that women do, the human race would've been extinct a long time ago."

I smiled.

He brushed a hair off my face. "You okay?"

"Yeah. I hope that doesn't happen too often though. The cleaning company was just here for the day. The thought of having my head in the toilet bowl after people use the stalls all night is enough to make me want to throw up again."

Rush smiled. "Hang on a second."

He got up and disappeared. Two minutes later he was back with a piece of paper and masking tape. He ripped two pieces off the roll and taped the paper onto the door of the stall I was still sitting in.

"There. Now this is your stall only."

I looked up and read what he'd written on the paper now taped to the door. OUT OF ORDER.

I laughed. "You can't put a stall out of order just in case I need to get sick."

"Like fuck I can't. It's my place. There're two other stalls. Anyone doesn't like it, they can come talk to me, and I'll tell 'em there's a whole ocean out back. Go piss in that." He extended his hand with a little silver tool that looked like an Allen key.

"What's that?" I asked.

"It's to open the door when the latch is closed, so you don't have to crawl underneath to use your clean stall. You just slip it through the crack in the door, and twist. It opens the latch. You'd be surprised how many little brats come in with their parents for dinner and think it's funny to go into a stall, lock it, and then crawl out underneath."

He was continuing to kill me with his kindness. It only made me want him more when I could no longer have him.

"Well, thank you. I really appreciate this."

"You're welcome." He lingered silently for a bit before he said, "Anyway...I, uh, hope you don't mind, I told my mother about the pregnancy. She wants you to know that you can call her anytime if you need to talk. I'll text you her info."

Wow.

I wasn't sure how I felt about Melody knowing, but something told me I was going to need to take her up on that.

VI KEELAND & PENELOPE WARD

"That's really nice of her. Thank you."

———

A few nights later, I was alone in my room having what felt like a panic attack. I'd gone to the doctor earlier in the day, and he told me that I was indeed pregnant. He scheduled me for my first ultrasound at the next appointment.

The formal news was no surprise, but it was still jarring to hear it confirmed beyond the shadow of a doubt.

The shock of my pregnancy was starting to wear off, and the reality was sinking in. Everything was starting to hit me at once.

The fact that I was going to be a mother.

The fact that I hadn't even told my dad yet.

Losing Rush. That was the hardest thing to accept. Well, maybe it would have been easier if I'd lost him totally. He was still around, making sure I was comfortable and safe at work, offering anything I needed when the only thing I really needed was his goddamn heart.

His being around made things even harder, because I yearned for more, for what we had—for him. I wanted nothing more than for him to hold me at night. I'd felt so safe in his arms. And now, just when I needed him most, I couldn't have him in that way, and it wasn't fair of me to expect it.

So, as I stared at Melody's beautiful sunset painting, which now stood for all of the hope that had been drained from my life, I realized I really needed to talk to someone. Feeling desperate, I looked up Rush's mom's contact information that he'd texted me and made the impulsive decision to call her.

After she answered, I said, "Melody?"

"Gia?"

She knew it was me. Rush must have told her to expect my call.

"Hi. I...uh...Rush told me it would be okay if I called you."

"Of course. He told me about your news. I would say congratulations, but I remember how that felt when people used to say it to me in the beginning. You don't feel ready for that because you're still harboring so much doubt about your abilities." She sighed into the phone. "Everything will be okay, Gia. I know it may not seem like that right now."

Her calming words made me even more emotional. *Is this what it's like to have a mother to talk to?*

I didn't waste any time getting to the point. "Would it be okay if I came to see you...to talk in person?"

"Of course. Are you sure you're feeling up to driving out here, because I could go there?"

"I'd actually like to come see you. I think I need to get out of town for a bit."

———

When I told Rush I was planning to go see his mother, he refused to let me drive my car, fearing it wouldn't make it all the way there.

He rented me a comfortable Honda CRV, despite my insistence that he not worry about me. But once on the freeway, I was grateful not to have to white knuckle my way through the ride.

On the way to Melody's, I grabbed a decaf tea from Starbucks and put on a romance audiobook about this hot Australian guy and a damn goat. The weather was perfect for a long ride, and it ended up being very relaxing, just what I needed to clear my head somewhat before seeing her.

Melody was gardening outside when I pulled into her driveway. She brushed the dirt off her smock and came over to the car. I rolled down the window.

"You made it in good time." She smiled.

"Yeah. Traffic was light."

We stepped inside. It was comforting to be back in her home, surrounded by all of the bright colors and paintings. Melody had a very Bohemian style, and there was a zen vibe throughout the place.

We sat down in her kitchen where she'd set up a fruit and cheese plate along with a large pitcher of lemonade.

I clasped my hands together and rested my elbows on the table. "Thank you for meeting me. I know how strange this must be...to be talking to your son's ex-girlfriend who's pregnant by someone else."

She shook her head as if to tell me my concerns were unfounded. "It's my pleasure, Gia. I was definitely surprised when Rush told me and a little disappointed, to be honest." She quickly placed her hand on mine to clarify. "Not in you...just in the fact that I knew what that might mean for you and my son."

Yeah.

I really hoped she wouldn't judge me because of how I'd gotten myself into this predicament—via a one-night stand. At least with Rush's dad, she'd been in an actual relationship, at least from her point of view.

"I don't know how much Rush told you..." I said.

"He told me everything. You don't have to explain anything to me about how it happened. I'm up to speed on that. Don't stress out over explaining a thing." She reached her hand across the table again, placing it on my arm. "How are you?"

Blowing out a shaky breath, I said, "Not too good. I feel guilty for feeling so sad—because that's no way to bring a child into this world. And I'm afraid that all of my negative energy will somehow affect the baby. But it's really hard to be happy when you feel like your world has turned upside down."

She looked sad for me. "I'm so sorry. But I assure you it's temporary. Things always get better, not necessarily *easy*, but better."

"Can you tell me a little about what your experience was like when you found out you were pregnant with Rush?"

Melody closed her eyes momentarily then said, "Well, you know, my situation wasn't that much different than yours. His father wasn't in the picture. I think what helped me in the beginning were a few things. Learning to take things one day at a time and understanding that you don't have to do more than that...is really key. It's all so overwhelming, that even thinking about it can be enough to make you go crazy. There are so many things you feel you need to do to prepare, but really the only thing you need to do right now is to breathe and to take care of yourself. There's no reason that you can't just take each moment as it comes. You don't have to deal with everything all at once, and you certainly don't have to have all of the answers."

Her words brought me a little comfort. "That's always easier said than done, but I will really try to remember that."

She gestured to the fruit platter. "Please have something to eat." Melody poured some of the lemonade into a glass and slid it in front of me. "The other thing is to understand that it's totally okay to not know what you're doing, to fly by the seat of your pants. There is a first time for everything, and a lot of it's going to be trial and error. Things like changing diapers, feeding the baby...it will all seem like second nature once you get used to it. But there's no real way to learn how to care for a baby aside from actually doing it. And again, no one expects you to be perfect out of the gate."

"Good. Because I am pretty sure I'll be a mess."

She laughed as she put a grape in her mouth. "You'll surprise yourself."

There was a moment of silence where she just looked at me from across the table. I don't know why I felt compelled to say, "I don't have a mother, you know."

Melody's eyes were brimming with sympathy. "I know."

"I couldn't remember if I told you that." I stared off, contemplating my lack of maternal role model. "How am I supposed to be good mother when I don't even have one?"

"Because it's innate," she said without hesitation. "You're a loving, caring person who will do everything in her power to care for her baby. She likely never had a motherly bone in her body. You're not your mother."

I truly hoped she was right. As I processed her words, tears ran down my cheeks. Melody moved her chair around to my side of the table and embraced me.

We stayed like that for a while until she gave me a napkin to wipe my eyes, then said, "It will be okay. It's hard to know that now. But trust me, it will." She got up and started walking toward her bedroom. "I'll be right back. I want to show you something."

A few minutes later, she returned with a photo album.

She planted it on the table. "I'm pretty sure Rush would kill me if he knew I was showing these to you, but that's too bad."

There were so many photos of a young Melody with baby Rush, who was surprisingly blond as a child. He still had the same naughty grin and expressive eyes. Melody looked so young, and her hair was really long.

When she came upon a set of photos that looked like they were professionally taken, she grinned from ear to ear.

"I remember this day." She covered her mouth as she pointed to a particular shot of baby Rush sitting on her lap. "Oh my gosh. I'd taken Rush to the Sears portrait studio. Right before this, he'd puked all over his brand-new outfit. I was in tears because the mall was quite a long drive for me, and I didn't want to have to come back, so the photographer gave me an outfit for him that a previous customer happened to leave behind. You see how his overalls are a little big?

"Look at that drooly, toothless smile," I gushed.

"I know I was so stressed out right before this, but once the photographer got us settled, Rush was hamming it up for the cameras. I left feeling so lucky, in a totally different mood compared to how I'd walked in." She gazed off into space for a moment before she looked at me. "That's what motherhood is like. It's a series of ups and downs. But it's all worth it, Gia. Trust me on that."

I kept staring at the image of baby Rush's big smile. It was reflective of the natural goodness built into my tough guy.

My tough guy.

Had I not gotten the memo that he wasn't mine anymore?

"What's wrong Gia?"

Melody must have noticed the sudden expression of sadness on my face. Damn pregnancy hormones.

The realization of it hit me like a ton of bricks. "I was falling in love with your son before this happened. Rush made it clear that he's not ready for all of this. I don't blame him. It just sucks, you know? Because he and I...we really had something. But I understand why he can't be with me. I do."

"I'm so sorry. If I had a magic button, I wish I could make this right for both of you. I wish my son felt differently, too. But if there's one thing I've learned about him, it's that I can't tell him what to do or how to feel. But I'll be rooting for you, that maybe he has a change of heart about it."

I wondered if she really meant that, or if deep inside she didn't want her son to be with someone who came with baggage when he could likely have anyone he wanted. I'd never know if she was telling me the truth or just wanted to make me feel better.

There was no way I was going to get my hopes up in any case. There was too much at stake now to worry about my broken heart. I needed to focus on the little heart beating inside of me instead.

CHAPTER 21

Rush

It had become my new nightly ritual. Standing outside of The Heights for several minutes at a time during peak hours. I'd be outside smoking while I watched things from afar through the windows.

When nightfall hit, the lights inside the restaurant gave me the perfect view of the hostess stand. The glare on the windows meant she couldn't see me watching her.

Being inside for long periods of time was too much for me lately. Plus, I needed to smoke even more, as if it were somehow going to take away this feeling that I couldn't even describe inside of my chest.

I would smoke cigarette after cigarette, alternating between nodding to patrons as they entered and peeking in the window to make sure Gia was okay, that she wasn't standing too much.

Everything had changed.

And yet *nothing* had changed.

I still *felt* everything I always had for her; the only difference was, I couldn't act on it anymore. That fucking killed me. It killed me to admit to her that I wasn't cut out for what she needed. It killed me to see the sadness in her eyes when I did. But I wasn't going to risk letting down a child. That's where I draw the line.

She would find her way eventually; she would. I just needed to help her land on her feet. Then, I'd encourage her to move back to the City once I knew she was gonna be okay—that *they* were gonna be okay. In the meantime, I wanted her here where I could keep an eye on her.

Smoke billowed out of my nose as I alternated between staring out at the water and over at Gia through the window.

I'd just put my butt out with my foot and blew out the last of it when I looked up to find two men lingering around the hostess station.

An alarm went off in my head. One guy was leaning into her and being too damn aggressive for my liking while the other just looked drunk, laughing like a fool.

A few minutes later, they were practically up her ass, blocking my view of her.

That's it.

I was done watching.

Storming inside, I charged over to where they were standing. "Can I help you with something?"

"No, we were just enjoying the company of your gorgeous hostess here."

"Well, she's not here for your enjoyment. She's doing her job. Give her some goddamn space."

Gia interjected, "Rush...it's really okay."

I ignored Gia's plea, vowing not to leave until they were out of her hair.

Both men refused to move from their spots.

I took two steps closer to them, clenching my first. "Did you not hear what the fuck I just said?"

"Dude, I heard you. I'm just not listening."

Then his friend made the mistake of getting up in my face with his beer-infused breath. "Who the fuck are you to tell him what to do?"

I completely snapped, grabbing the man by the neck and dragging him with all of my might out the door onto the street. The other guy followed us outside.

"I own this place, motherfucker, and I can do whatever I want," I spat in his face before releasing him from my death grip.

Oak, who had been up on the rooftop when all of this went down, came running outside.

"Keep these guys out," I spewed before brushing past him without giving any further explanation.

All eyes were on me as I walked back inside. Not the most professional decision of my career. But that was the last thing I was worried about at the moment.

Gia looked alarmed as she returned from seating some customers. "Don't you think that was a bit of an overreaction?"

"No," I bit out. "Now get back to work."

I spent the rest of the night alone in my office ruminating. While I didn't regret throwing those assholes out, it was the bigger picture of what it represented that was eating away at me.

If I was gonna stay away from Gia, I had to stop being so emotionally invested in her—so damn possessive. It was a hard habit to break.

It was just before closing. I suddenly jumped out of my seat and walked through the restaurant without making eye contact with Gia or Oak.

I ventured straight out into the parking lot, got into my car, lit a cigarette then grabbed my phone. I scrolled down to her name.

Was I really doing this?
I needed to.
I typed out a text.

Rush: You around to fuck?

Barely a few seconds passed before a response came in.

Everly: What makes you think I'm still talking to you after the shit you pulled last time, standing me up.

Rush: Is that a no?

Everly: I wish I could say no to you.

Rush: I'm heading to your place.

Everly: I'll be here.

I must have been going ninety miles per hour the entire way to her house. It wasn't out of excitement to see her. I knew it was because a part of me wanted to get this over with, just to prove I could move on from Gia. Because I *had* to.

Everly opened the door dressed in nothing but Daisy Duke denim shorts and a bra. I walked past her without so much as a greeting, heading straight toward her fridge where I helped myself to one of the beers I knew she kept fully stocked there.

"Well, hello to you, too." She laughed, leaning over the counter, her tits on full display.

After downing half of the bottle, I walked over to where she was standing.

Everly wrapped her arms around my neck. "I'm really glad you called. It's been too long."

The old Rush would have been pounding her against the wall by now. I just stood there staring at her with my body rigid, unsure if I could really go through with this.

It felt like I was cheating on Gia, and I could honestly say it was the first time in my life that I'd ever given a fuck about something like that.

She stepped back. "You're sweating bullets. What's going on with you tonight?"

My eyes trailed down her body. There was no doubt that Everly was sexy as hell. I shouldn't have been overthinking this so much. But I wasn't even hard because I was so freaking stressed.

"I think I know just what you need," she said, dropping to her knees.

She began to unzip my jeans as she licked her lips readying to give me head.

I froze.

Taking my cock into her hand, she leaned in to take me into her mouth when I yanked on the back of her hair just before her lips were able to make contact with my skin.

"Fuck," I groaned as I let her go and zipped up my pants.

She stood up and glared at me. "What the fuck is going on with you, Rush? Seriously. You're the one who texted *me*. What kind of a game are you playing?"

I knew between tonight and the last time I stood her up, if I walked out that door, I could pretty much kiss any hope of meaningless sex in the future with Everly goodbye. That fact didn't mean shit to me...so off I went.

I just couldn't go through with it.

This wasn't a need for sex. This was a test. And I'd fucking failed.

Stopping in the doorway, I finally apologized. "I'm sorry."

"Get the fuck out. And don't even think about ever calling or texting me again." She slammed the door in my face.

Her words didn't faze me as I walked back out and got into my car. I didn't start it right away, just stayed there staring out at the desolate street.

My behavior tonight blew me away.

Unlike the ride to Everly's, I was driving back at a slower than average speed. That was probably because a part of me knew I wasn't headed home.

After I parked, I must have sat in my car for over thirty minutes deciding whether or not to ring her doorbell.

What the fuck are you doing, Rush?
Why are you here?
My phone chimed.

Gia: Is there any reason why you're parked outside of my house?

Rush: Stakeout?

Gia: Not buying it.

Rush: Pizza delivery?

Gia: My pizza must be awfully cold then.

Rush: I don't know what I'm doing here.

Gia: Do you want to come in?

Rush: Yes.

Gia: But you won't...

Rush: I don't think I should.

Gia: Okay.

Despite my words, a few moments later, I was at the door knocking.

Gia opened, wearing a thin, white nightgown that showed off her enormous nipples. I had to pry my eyes upward because all I wanted to do was lift the material up and suck on them so badly.

It was quiet in the house as I looked around. "Where are your roommates?"

"Every one of them either is out or working. That rarely happens. I'm enjoying the peace and quiet."

This wasn't good. I really needed to leave.

She surprised me when she said, "Will you have some ice cream with me?"

"Ice cream..."

"Yeah." She smiled, and I just melted at the sight of it.

Seemed innocent enough.

"Depends on the flavor," I teased.

"Chunky Monkey...kind of like I'm gonna look in a few months?"

That thought should have turned me off, maybe, but it had the opposite effect. I loved her new curves and the idea of more. My affinity for her body only made my situation all that much harder.

"That's my favorite flavor," I said.

We sat in the living room, quietly eating out of the same container of Ben & Jerry's.

She finally said, "Everyone was talking about your outburst earlier, how you threw those two guys out and then how you just left The Heights without saying anything to anyone."

My mouth was full of ice cream. "Well, let them talk. I don't care. I still stand by what I did. Those pricks had no place hovering around you like that."

"Where did you go when you left?"

When I stopped eating and didn't say anything, she drew her own conclusion. Maybe my guilt was obvious.

A look of worry flashed across her face. "You went to see a woman?" When I didn't answer, she became more insistent. "Answer me."

I still didn't want to admit my stupidity tonight.

She continued to push, "You had sex with someone tonight?"

"No." It came out louder than I'd intended.

"Then where were you?"

I didn't want to lie to her.

"I tried to hook up with someone. I wanted to forget—forget about what happened at The Heights, forget about you."

I hadn't meant to be so blunt. But she wanted the truth. That was it.

Tears started to fall from her eyes. It fucking killed me that I was upsetting her. Why did I tell her the truth?

"But I couldn't, Gia."

"Why not? You might as well. It's not like you owe me anything. You should be out having a fuckfest right now. You made your decision when it comes to me."

"That's not fair."

"It's the truth!"

"Just because I can't be with you, doesn't mean I don't *want* to be with you. And it doesn't mean I'm ready to move on, as much as I wish I could. Staying away from you is the hardest fucking thing I've ever had to do."

We were both silent for the longest time, just staring intensely into each other's eyes.

"I miss you," she whispered.

I miss you, too.

I couldn't resist bringing her into me. She buried her face in my chest. My heart was beating out of control. It was all too much: the softness of her skin, the recognition of her scent. The need to pick up exactly where we'd left off.

My dick hardened. I couldn't get it up for Everly, but put this gorgeous, pregnant women in my arms, and my body was fully awakened. I wished her being pregnant turned me off, but I'd never been more turned on by anything in my life.

Coming inside the house was a mistake.

I let go of her, placing my spoon on the coffee table and standing up. "I have to go."

As I was walking out the door, her voice stopped me. "I have my first ultrasound tomorrow."

I froze. My heart started to pound faster. Hearing her say that really made it hit home that there was an actual *human being* inside of her.

She continued, "I'm really scared. Like what if they find something wrong...or there's no heartbeat...or I freak out when I see it. I know this is going to sound crazy, Rush. Besides Riley, who's out of state this week, you're the best friend I have here. I haven't even mustered the courage to tell my father yet. Anyway...do you think you could come with me?"

What?

Say something.

"I don't know, Gia."

"Please?"

How could I say no? She was scared, and aside from all of the complicated parts to this situation, I cared deeply for this girl. If she needed me to hold her hand, then I needed to suck it up and do it.

I let out a long breath and nodded. "Okay."

CHAPTER 22

Rush

"**Y**ou're making me even more nervous." Gia rested her hand on my knee, stopping the incessant bob up and down of my leg. I hadn't even realized I was doing it.

"Sorry."

Sitting side by side in the doctor's office waiting room, I impatiently waited for her name to be called. I'd been a wreck from the time we pulled into the damn parking lot. Some help I was. I'd come because she was nervous, yet here she was having to calm me down. I had no idea why I felt so anxious, but ten minutes ago when the receptionist's phone rang, I literally jumped right out of my chair. I'd had to cover by pretending I needed to use the bathroom. *What the fuck is wrong with me?*

"I was thinking about my old job last night," Gia said. "All the greeting cards that I wrote the copy for."

"Oh yeah? Bet you didn't get your own bathroom stall at that job."

She laughed. "No, I definitely didn't. But I wasn't comparing my old job to working for you. There's no comparison to how much more I enjoy spending time with you at The Heights...I mean, working at The Heights. But I was thinking about the cards I used to write that were meant to congratulate people on their pregnancies. At the time, I thought they were funny. Although, right now, as I'm sitting in an actual obstetrician's office, I'm thinking maybe some of them went a little too far, almost to the point of being insensitive without even realizing it."

"Like what?"

"Well, this one in particular I remember writing went something like this: On the outside it said, '*How do you fit a watermelon through a donut hole?*' And then on the inside it said, '*You're about to find out.*'

I chuckled. "That's funny."

"Says the man who doesn't have to push a watermelon through his donut hole."

The receptionist called Gia's name, and she looked over at me. The fear was suddenly palpable in her eyes. I took her hand and squeezed. "It's going to be fine. This baby is going to be healthy and beautiful just like his mom."

"His?"

"His what?"

"You said just like *his* mom. So you think I'm having a boy?"

I hadn't noticed I'd given the baby a sex. "Come on. Stop stalling." I stood and gave her hand a slight tug. "And I don't *think* you're having a boy, I *know* what you're having."

Gia stood. "You do?"

I winked. "Of course. A giant fucking watermelon."

———

"It's a little early to be able to tell the sex of the baby. But, before I start, do you want to know if I'm able to see the gender clearly?" The sonogram technician pulled gloves from a box on the counter and snapped them onto her hands.

"Umm." Gia looked at me for an answer. "I don't know. I didn't think you could tell this soon, so I really haven't given it any thought. What do you think, Rush?"

I smirked. "Up to you. I already know what it is."

The sonogram technician obviously didn't know that I meant she was pregnant with a watermelon. She flicked off the lights in the room and pulled up a stool next to Gia. "So Dad already thinks he knows what it is, huh? I'm guessing that means he thinks it's a boy. Most dads do."

Gia got flustered. "He's not...he thinks it's a..."

I attempted to help her. "I'm not the...uh...I don't think..."

The technician must've been used to two tongue-tied people in this room. "I'll tell you what. I won't tell you what you're having if I can see, but I'll note it in your chart so that you can call the office at any time if you decide to find out."

Gia let out a loud rush of air. "Okay. Yeah. That's great."

"I'm going to just untie your gown and pull it up to access your belly, and we might need to roll down your pants a little bit."

"Okay."

Gia squeezed my hand as the technician got her ready. I might be a sick fuck, but my cock twitched at the sight of the smooth skin on her stomach. It was apparently oblivious we were at a medical appointment and not a peep show. The technician rolled down Gia's leggings to just above her pubic bone, and my eyes stayed glued to her tanned skin.

Fuck. I want to defile a mother.

The technician held up a tube of something. "This might be a little cold." She then proceeded to squirt some gel shit all over Gia's belly.

Here let me take care of that for you. My lube will be nice and warm.

I shook my head to rid the thought.

It didn't help one fucking bit.

The tech pulled a monitor on wheels next to the examination table and positioned it so that the three of us could see. I stayed on the opposite side, next to Gia's head so we had the same view.

The minute she touched the wand to Gia's belly, a loud sound came out of the machine. The technician looked at the screen and adjusted a knob. "Your baby has a nice strong heartbeat."

Gia and I stared at the screen.

"I'll give you a quick tour of the baby's anatomy so that you can enjoy it while I take measurements and the pictures I need." The technician pointed to what looked like a string of pearls. "This is your baby's spine." She tilted the wand a little to the left with one hand and pointed to the screen with the other. The image was grainy and black and white, but I could make out what she showed next before she even said it. "Head." She outlined what was clearly a skull, then traced down the baby's profile. "Nose. Lips." *Holy crap.* I could actually see an outline of a baby's face. Although it looked more like an alien swimming than a baby from where I stood. But there it was, a person—inside of Gia—one with its own heartbeat and profile already. The technician smiled and moved the wand around a lot while looking at the screen. "You have an active one. It's turning around a lot." Just as she said that, something very clear came into view.

"Is that a hand?" Gia said.

"Sure is."

"Wow."

"If you opt to have a 3D sonogram later in your pregnancy, the pictures are really clear. But you're actually getting a pretty nice show today considering you're only fourteen weeks."

Mesmerized by the screen, I'd completely forgotten about Gia's stomach, and it hit me that I was actually excited about the pregnancy for the first time. I couldn't wait to meet the little guy.

Okay, so maybe I *did* think he was a boy.

I continued to stare in awe. I saw fingers move, toes, lips, a long neck and was that...

My excitement must've gotten the best of me. I pointed to what I thought was a penis. "Is that his..."

The technician laughed. "No. That's actually a whole foot."

Gia had turned her head and was watching me instead of the screen. Her face glowed and she looked so beautiful. Without giving it any thought, I leaned down and kissed her forehead. "Okay. So maybe *I do* sort of think it's a boy."

The technician finished scanning Gia's belly and then printed off a few pictures. "First refrigerator pictures, Mom," she said handing them to Gia. "I'm not supposed to give any results or anything, but everything looks great. Why don't you get dressed, and I'll have the group PA pop in to answer any questions you might have today since you're not due to see the doctor at this visit." She handed a bunch of paper towels to Gia. "To clean up the gel."

"Okay. Thank you."

The technician left us alone in the room, and Gia wiped a few tears, then began to wipe off her belly. I took the paper towels from her hand and cleaned up the mess. It had seemed perfectly natural to do, but after I'd done it, I noticed Gia was looking at me funny. "I could've done that."

I tossed the paper towels in the garbage, and when I turned back around, Gia sat up on the exam table. Her gown that had been untied and pushed up, fell open. She had on a black lacy bra, and her tits were practically spilling out of the cups. Gia traced what my eyes were glued to and looked down. "I've gained six pounds so far, and it all seems to have went to my boobs."

I swallowed. "Pregnancy definitely agrees with you."

She put her hand on her belly. "I'm not looking forward to getting fat."

Apparently her swollen breasts made me delirious. Because the thought of a curvy Gia with a big, round, full belly and a little sag to her perky tits actually had me getting hard in the doctor's office. "You're going to be fucking sexy pregnant."

She thought I was trying to make her feel better. Standing from the exam table, she pointed to the chair behind me. "You'll have to keep lying to me as I start to waddle. Can you hand me my shirt?"

Even though her gown had just been wide open, Gia turned her back to me to change into her shirt. She wasn't normally modest about her body, so it made me think she really did think she wasn't attractive pregnant.

A knock at the door came before I could set her straight. The PA entered and extended her hand to both of us. "I'm Jessica Abbot. I'll be seeing you from time to time over the course of your pregnancy. Usually it's after a sonogram or calling you with lab results. I just took a quick look at your sonogram and everything is measuring to the due date we originally anticipated. Your baby looks happy and healthy. Are there any questions you have for me today, about the sonogram or otherwise?"

Gia shook her head. "I don't think so, no."

"Okay. Well, you can keep up with your regular, non-pregnancy activities. Work, sleep, sex—all as usual."

Gia glanced at me and then to the PA. "Is it normal for pregnancy to...affect your libido?"

"Yes. Very. Many women experience a decrease in their sex drive during their pregnancy. Often it's in the first trimester and then it comes back with a vengeance toward the end."

"Oh."

I looked over at Gia. Her face was turning pink. She was embarrassed to ask something...maybe because I was standing next to her. I pointed to the door. "Do you want me to give you two a minute to talk?"

Gia shook her head before taking a deep breath, then turned back to the PA and said, "I think I have the opposite problem."

The PA smiled. "Oh. I'm sorry. I misread what you were asking. Yes, it's definitely normal to have a heightened sex drive. Every woman's experience is individual to that particular pregnancy, and some will have an increased sexual appetite that fluctuates, whereas others might have no desire for the entire pregnancy. But you're young and healthy, so there's no reason not to enjoy yourself if the urge is stronger than normal."

Fuck. Gia just told this woman that she was horny. All. The. Time.

"So...*any* kind of sex is okay then? I won't hurt the baby?"

What the hell was she getting at?

"As long as you aren't physically challenging yourself too much, yes. Your partner won't hurt the baby, if that's what your fear is." She glanced at me and then back to Gia. "It's actually a common concern in couples. So I'm glad you're asking if it's been weighing on your mind."

Gia bit her bottom lip. Her pink face turned bright red now. "What about sex...without a partner?" She motioned between the two of us. "We're not... and I wanted to ask my doctor at the last appointment, but he's a man and he's older...and I'd like to use a...."

While I was completely lost on what the hell Gia was getting at, apparently the secret code she was speaking made sense to the PA. "*Oh.* I'm sorry. Yes, absolutely. You can safely use a vibrator or any other toys that you'd regularly use. Not an issue at all." The woman dug into her pocket and pulled out a business card. "I totally understand why asking that question to Dr. Daniels might've been difficult. He's a wonderful doctor, but I get it. Please...call me any time you want to discuss anything."

The two of them chatted away for a few more minutes, but I didn't hear a fucking word of it. My brain was totally stuck on the fact that Gia was horny and about to go to town on herself with her vibrator.

CHAPTER 23

Gia

"Is everything okay?" Rush hadn't said one word since leaving the doctor's office, and we were halfway to my house.

"Fine."

"Did it freak you out to go with me? I'm sorry if it was too much to ask."

"No. I appreciate you asking me."

Seeing his knuckles turn white from the death grip he had on the steering wheel and listening to his curt responses didn't make me feel like he *appreciated* going.

I stared down at the ultrasound pictures and tried to talk myself into believing that I was paranoid and that nothing was wrong. But I felt like I'd made a big mistake relying on Rush. It was a lot to ask of anyone, and I really needed to learn to stand on my own two feet. For the last few weeks, I'd been weighing the pros and cons on Rush's offer to help me, to stay at his house until after the baby was born. Today made me realize it wasn't a good idea. He had a big heart, and I believed that his offer was sincere, but it was unfair to burden anyone with my problems. I needed to set him free. As much as the thought gutted me, I knew it was the right thing to do. Like having a covered wound that hurts when you touch it, once I'd decided it was time to rip the Band-Aid off, I thought it best to do it in one quick tear. So when we pulled up to the house, I took a deep breath and turned to face Rush.

"I've been doing a lot of thinking lately. And although your offer was extremely generous, I'm not going to be staying out here after our summer share is up."

Rush had been staring out the window straight ahead even after he'd pulled to the curb. He finally turned to me. "What? Why?"

"I need to do this myself, Rush. If I'm here with you, I'm going to just keep leaning on you, and that's not fair to either of us."

He looked back and forth between my eyes. "I want you to lean on me."

I touched his arm. "I know you do. Because you're a good man, Rush. But it's only going to make it harder to walk away at some point. And I *will* keep you from moving on. Look at what happened the other night when you tried to be with another woman. You're the most loyal man I've ever met. I realize now that you aren't going to move on with me out here, even though you want to. And, honestly, neither will I." I felt tears welling in my eyes. "So I think it's time. Sometimes you have to let go of the things you never really had."

Rush's head hung with his eyes shut, so I used the opportunity to get out of the car before he saw me break down. "Thanks for taking me today, Rush."

I made it to the door holding back my emotions, but by the time I tried to put the key in the lock, the unshed tears had blurred my vision, and I dropped my keys on the floor. I bent down, but a large hand scooped them up before I could.

Rush's voice was close behind me when I stood, but I couldn't turn around.

"I'm an idiot," he said with a strained low voice. It made my tears fall faster. I stared straight ahead at the door.

"No. You're not. I'm the idiot."

"You said I'm the most loyal man you've ever met. That's my biggest fear. That I can't live up to that. That part of me is just like my father. You see me the way you want to see me. Not as a man who's fucked a dozen different women each summer and never wondered that I might be hurting them in the wake of walking out the door the next morning."

I turned around and found tears in Rush's eyes, too. Reaching up, I wiped one cheek with my thumb, then the other. "They were consenting adults. You didn't promise them anything or lead them on. Loyalty is pledging the truth to yourself and others. You were always truthful in what you wanted from them. But what you've given me is also your truth, and it's because you are so loyal that I have to be the one to walk away." I put my hand over his heart. "You pledged to be there for me in here. And if I stay, you will be. Because your loyalty is unwavering. That's the reason I have to go, because it's your loyalty that won't let you be the person to walk away."

Rush looked down and took a few deep breaths. I knew showing me how vulnerable he is wasn't easy, so I didn't push. When he looked back up, he stared straight into my eyes. "You've always really had it."

"Your loyalty?"

He shook his head. "You said, *sometimes you have to let go of the things you never really had.* You've had my love since day one. You've had *me* since day one. I was just too chicken-shit to admit it."

My heart started to beat faster. I tried to stop it, afraid of allowing myself to get my hopes up for fear that he was saying something other than what I wanted to think he meant. But inside of my chest thundered like a runaway train.

Rush cupped both my cheeks. "Gia Mirabelli, I'm so fucking in love with you, that I can't think straight. There's no way in hell I'm letting you leave. Not from this house. Not from The Heights. Not from my life. It scares the shit out of me, but I realized today seeing that little boy on the screen, that I'm not just in love with you. I'm in love with that little alien you have growing inside of you already. I want it all. I want the fucked-up dolls in my closets. I want to hold your hair back when you're puking your brains out. I want to eat Chunky Monkey with you out of the container while we lie in bed naked at two in the morning. And I definitely, most definitely, want to be the one to take care of you when you have a heightened sexual appetite."

Tears streamed down my face. Of all the things he'd just pledged, for some stupid reason, I got stuck on the ice cream. Maybe it's because deep down I already knew he wanted to hold my hair back and take care of me, but I thought he might be nuts for thinking he was going to want me as the months passed. "I'm going to be big and fat from all that Chunky Monkey."

He took a step closer and ran his hand along the curve of my hip. "Bring it on. I've been imagining you about fifty pounds heavier and round while I jerked off the last few days. I think I might keep you that way after the pregnancy."

I laughed, yet as crazy as he sounded, I knew he was telling me the truth. "I think you're a little insane."

His beautiful face turned serious again. "I'm sorry I've been pushing you away and making you feel bad. But I'm done being a pussy. I want you despite all of my own fears that have nothing to do with you, and despite the fact that you probably deserve someone better than me. Please forgive me, and tell me you'll stay and be with me. Really *be* with me this time."

I didn't have to think about the question. Although I probably should've given him some warning that my response was going to be more than just vocal. I jumped up and into Rush's arms, causing him to stumble back a few steps and almost fall as he staggered off the front porch. "Yes! Yes!" I planted a kiss on his teeth when he opened his mouth to laugh.

Shaking his head, he said, "Can we move this inside now? I'm thinking it's about time we seal the deal on this relationship."

"What the hell is wrong with you?" I looked at myself in the bathroom mirror. I'd told Rush to make himself comfortable while I locked myself into the bathroom to get control of my nerves. I'd been with this man. He'd already seen my body naked and went down on me. And not ten minutes ago he'd professed his love for me and the unborn child of another man. Yet I was literally shaking. I brushed my teeth, rinsed my mouth and stared at my reflection a few more minutes. "He said he loves you. Now what are you waiting for?"

A soft knock came at the door. "Everything okay in there?"

"Yes. I'll be right out."

Ten minutes later, when I was still inside trying to will my legs to leave the bathroom, there was another knock at the door. "Gia?"

It sounded like he was right on the other side of the door. I walked over and leaned my head against it from this side. "Yeah."

"I'm nervous, too. If it helps any."

My shoulders loosened. "You are?"

"Yep. You scare the living shit out of me."

I smiled, but still didn't open the door. "Why are we so scared of each other right now, Rush?"

"Because when you finally accept that you found *the one*, it's terrifying that you might lose them and then there'd never be another."

I think my heart actually swelled in my chest a little. "Oh my God. That's the most romantic thing I've ever heard anyone say."

"Oh yeah?" he said. "Well, come out here and let me *do* romantic things to you, beautiful."

Taking a deep breath, I unlocked the door and opened it. His smile made my knees weak as he extended his hand to me. Placing my hand in his felt monumental, like it was my heart I was surrendering. Rush had been so sweet, so open, yet none of those things made me relax like when he abruptly yanked my hand and tugged me against him hard. The little rough around the edges felt like my Rush again. *My Rush.*

Pressed up against him, he brought both my hands behind my back and locked them there in one of his. His other hand gripped the back of my neck, and his mouth sealed over mine.

I yelped between our joined lips when Rush scooped me into his arms and carried me over to the bed. Somehow we managed not to break the kiss while he set me down and climbed on top of me. All of the nerves I'd felt just a few minutes ago were pushed out by the carnal desire I felt for this man. The kiss that had started off warm and tender, quickly heated to hot and wild. Rush used one knee to nudge my legs open and then ground his hips down. The feel of his hard cock pressing against my center made me moan. I couldn't wait for him to be inside of me.

Sensing my need, Rush broke the kiss and pulled back. My head was literally dizzy. He never broke our gaze as he tugged off his shirt and then slipped mine over my head. His tongue ran along his bottom lip as he looked down at my bra. When his gaze returned to meet mine, he swallowed before speaking. "Do you need gentle, baby?"

I shook my head.

A wicked grin spread across his face. "Thank fuck."

Rush shed the rest of our clothes so fast that it felt like one of his hands stripped me and the other ripped off his pants. Settling back on top of me, he rubbed his bare cock up and down between my legs, and then pressed hard against my clit. I thought I might come from just the friction. The gleam in his eyes told me he knew exactly what he was doing to me. But two could play his game. I spread my legs as wide as they could go and slipped my hand down between us to grab him. Realizing my hand couldn't wrap fully around his girth, I was thankful how much this man turned me on because I was ready for all of him.

Our eyes were locked as he pushed inside. He rocked his hips, easing his hard, thick, length in and out a few times. I gasped when he bore down and sank deep inside of me.

Rush stilled, and I felt his body begin to shake. "Fuck, Gia. *Fuck.* This is where I've wanted to be since the day I met you. Deep inside you, just like you are inside of me."

He took my mouth in the most beautiful kiss as he glided in and out and then returned to watching me. The green of his eyes darkened to near gray as his thrusts became more and more powerful. I had sex before, but never knew until that moment that I'd never been made love to. Our bodies became one, but it was our hearts and souls connecting that made the act so much more than physical. Everything else in the world ceased to exist except us.

Rush's jaw clenched and he growled, "I want to fill up this sweet pussy over and over again, every fucking day."

That was it. Whatever last bit of control I had was completely annihilated hearing the desperation in his voice. Waves began to crest. My entire body hummed with need. Tears of joy crowded my eyes. Rush reached down and lifted one of my thighs into the air allowing him to drive even deeper into my body. I moaned as my orgasm ripped through me, and Rush responded by fucking me harder and harder. He roared as he bucked one last time and planted himself as deep as he could possibly go before coming inside of me.

After, he kissed me gently as he continued to move in and out, telling me how beautiful I was and how much he loved me. It dawned on me that I hadn't told him it back. Even though I was certain he knew, it was time. "Rush?" I whispered.

"Hmmm?" He trailed a path of tender kisses from my ear down to my neck and then up and over my chin before our lips met.

"I love you, too."

His smile split from ear to ear. "Well, that's good. Because I love you, too. But not Tee-Oh-Oh, too." He climbed down my body and planted a kiss on my belly. "Because I love you, Tee-W-Oh, two."

CHAPTER 24

Rush

I loved exploring her when she was fast asleep. As I circled my index finger around her nipple, I swore her areola looked bigger and darker than yesterday. Her body was changing every day, like a flower slowly blooming. And fuck...I loved it so much. I loved *Gia* so much.

Making this kind of commitment to someone was scary as all fuck, but I wouldn't have had it any other way. Accepting my feelings was the best thing I ever did. It felt so good not to have to fight them anymore. The fear hadn't gone away. The difference was that I was letting it be there, telling it to fuck off while I lived my life and loved this girl. While I was more scared than I had ever been in my life, I'd never been happier, either. And that trumped everything else.

I slid my hand slowly down her abdomen before slipping my fingers inside of her. She was wet. Gia's sexual appetite was voracious, even in her sleep.

Her body stirred and then she reached out to me. "Hey...you trying to get some?"

I slowly pulled my fingers out of her. "I am. You givin'?"

She climbed on top of me, kissing me hard on the lips. "I thought you might be tired of me after all the times we did it last night."

"Fuck no. "I squeezed her ass. "Did you know there's something called preggophilia?"

"Oh my God...what?"

"It's a fetish. I Googled *can't get enough of pregnant woman* and that came up. I think I might be a preggophile."

She was cracking up. "I thought you were just saying that at first, but I'm starting to believe it."

I took her hand and placed it on my rigid cock. "Believe *this.*"

Gia straddled me before sliding my cock into her wet cunt. The feeling of sinking into her hot pussy was like no other. It was truly like what I imagined heaven felt like.

She started to grind her hips over me. I loved sex with her in any position, but when she rode me, it always felt like I was even deeper into her. I loved being able to watch her tits bounce and to place my hands over different parts of her body, exploring her face, her hips, her ass. It almost made me feel guilty to be able to sit back while she did all the work, except for the fact that she really seemed to love being on top, seemed to love being in control.

You know what else I freaking loved? Being able to fuck her without a condom. Before her, I never took chances with anyone—always covered it up. Fucking her bare felt almost *too good*, and I had to constantly try to stop myself from prematurely blowing my load. Thankfully, Gia was so horny that she never took very long to come.

This time was no exception. As she came crashing down on top of me, throbbing over my cock, I spilled inside of her until there was nothing left.

Gia collapsed onto my chest. "How did I ever get so lucky?"

I caressed her hair for a while before I said, "I'm the lucky one."

We lay there in silence. I don't know what made me say, "I feel sorry for that bastard from The Heights, whoever he is, because he won't know what he's missing out on." I blew out a breath. "Fuck that. I don't feel sorry for him. I'm glad he took off."

She laid her head on me and was quiet for a while before she said, "I wish this baby was yours. I would give anything for that."

Her words squeezed at my chest. Of course, I wished that were the case. But dwelling on it in any way was futile. We could never change the fact that it wasn't mine.

"I wish that, too, for ego reasons, but you know...he won't ever feel like he doesn't have a father. I'll always be there for him—and for you. In the end, it won't make a difference who his sperm donor was." I held her tighter. "Things are the way they were meant to be. You don't meet people by accident in life. That dude was meant to leave, and you were meant to meet me. It's all written in the stars."

She lifted her head to meet my eyes. "I didn't know you were so philosophical."

"Have you *met* my mother?"

She chuckled. "That's true."

When her smile faded, I asked, "What's wrong?"

She rubbed her stomach. "Pretty soon, we're not gonna be able to hide this. How do I explain it to the people at work?"

"You don't have to explain shit to them. You don't owe anyone an explanation."

"But I want to do it before they start talking. I feel like I just need to lay it all out on the line and be the one to control when they find out before they start whispering about my size."

I didn't want this to stress her out and vowed to myself that I would take care of things.

"Don't worry about any of that. I'll handle it."

———

The next day at The Heights, I called a mandatory staff meeting right after closing. I wanted everyone there so that I didn't have to explain myself twice. If employees weren't on shift, they were still called in and paid for the hour.

I specifically did it during Gia's night off, so that she didn't have to deal with it.

Everyone gathered around me. I'd chosen the downstairs bar area as the site of our informal meeting. People were definitely confused. I think they might have thought I was closing down The Heights, because it was unlike mc to call a meeting.

When it looked like everyone was there, I cleared my throat to get their attention. "I'm gonna make this brief. I know you're all tired, and it's late, so I'm not keeping you a second longer than I have to." I took a deep breath. "You know I don't normally talk about my personal life, because it generally has nothing to do with business, but because Gia is an employee here, I don't want her to have to worry about people talking behind her back." I inhaled before spitting it out. "She and I are together. She's my girlfriend." I paused. "I love her. And we're also having a baby. If you have any questions or concerns about that news, you can see me. But I don't want anyone making her feel uncomfortable because of it or treating her any differently—unless it's to make her job easier." I nodded once. "I have nothing more to say. You guys have a good night."

I walked away, leaving the rumblings and whispers of my staff behind. No one had a chance to congratulate me or even respond. That was fine with me.

Large footsteps trailed me. I knew exactly who it was before his deep voice came up from behind me. "Whoa. Whoa. Whoa. You think you're gonna make an announcement like that and not have to deal with me? You got another thing coming."

As Oak followed me into my office, I couldn't help the smile on my face because I knew he was gonna have a field day with this.

I turned to face him and sighed. "I'm sorry I didn't tell you first. I went to find you earlier, but you were busy breaking up that fight and then the night just flew by."

"This is for real?" He smiled.

"Yeah. It's for real."

Oak caught me off guard when he approached and gave me a huge bear hug. "I couldn't be happier for you, man. How far along is she?"

I wracked my brain for an answer I hoped would make sense.

"A couple months..."

A couple months—ish.

"You guys have been together for a while, then. You had me fooled. It explains a lot about your crazy behavior, though."

"We've been keeping it on the down low until we figured things out."

He placed his hand on my shoulder. "Fatherhood is a gift. I'm glad you'll get to experience it. I was worried you wouldn't because you're stubborn."

"It wasn't something I ever thought I wanted, Oak. But I guess when you meet the right person, that changes everything."

"Damn straight." He just kept shaking his head and smiling. "I knew from day one that you and Gia would end up together. I'm glad you finally saw it, too."

That night on my way home, I went to light up a cigarette. For the first time, I really stopped to think about the fact that I needed to quit because of the baby. I couldn't smoke around him and couldn't be smoking around Gia anymore, either. Throwing the unlit butt out the window, I decided to give quitting a real honest try this time.

Then, I picked up the phone and dialed Gia. When she picked up, I simply said, "You know that work situation you were worried about? I took care of it."

—————

A few nights later, Gia and I were headed out to eat when I said, "Do you mind if we stop by my house real quick?"

"No, not at all. You know I love your house."

I hadn't asked her to move in with me. We were together every night, sometimes at my place, sometimes at hers. But I didn't want to push things. Still, I wanted her to know that I was all-in, so I spent a good chunk of this week putting together a little surprise for her.

When we entered my place, I led her toward the spare bedroom. "I want to show you something."

She looked suspicious when she grinned. "Okay..." When I opened the door, she gasped. "No way!"

"I spent the week changing the guest room into a nursery. Do you like it?"

She got a load of the newly decorated space. My mother had painted a mural on the wall of the moon and stars. I'd assembled a white crib and the whole room was done up in blues and grays to match the wall. A changing table sat in the corner. It was fully stocked with supplies. The room was move-in ready.

She walked around, soaking it all in. "I...I love it. Did you design this all yourself?"

"I might have gotten a little help from my mother. She painted this wall, actually. She's been out here all week, and you didn't even know. But I picked out the bedding and the other stuff. I figured it's pretty gender-neutral with the gray mixed in...just in case he turns out to be a girl."

She was pretty speechless.

"I don't know what to say. This is the most amazing thing that anyone has ever done for me."

Kissing her on the forehead, I said, "I don't want you to think I'm pressuring you to move in. That's not what this is about. This room is for the baby whether you're living apart from me or with me. That's your choice. But I figured he's gonna need a place to sleep when you're here."

There was nothing I wanted more than for Gia to move into my place. But she's very independent, and I didn't want to pressure her. There were enough changes happening. At the same time, I wanted her to know that my home was her home.

Gia walked over to the corner of the room and grabbed a stuffed bear that was sitting in the rocking chair. She hugged it and shocked me when she started to cry.

She wiped her eyes. "Is it weird that I just don't feel deserving of all of this?"

"Why not?"

"Just a few weeks ago, I felt like my life was over, like I was going to have to start from scratch and find my way back up. Then, you told me that you loved me and would accept my baby and me. And it just...it turned my world right side up again. Accepting my child as your own is a huge undertaking. I feel like you're giving me so much, sacrificing so much, and all I have to give you is my love."

Wrapping my hands around her face, I looked into her eyes. "That's all I need. It's something that only a few people have truly given me in this life. You underestimate how much that really means to me." I led her over to the rocker and pulled her onto my lap. "You never know when the tables will turn in life, Gia, or what will happen. But I know that if something unimaginable *did* happen, that you'd do anything for me. And when it comes to you and this baby...yes, it's a huge undertaking...but sacrifice isn't the right word—it's an honor."

CHAPTER 25

Gia

It was the third black dress I'd tried on in ten minutes. I pulled it over my head and threw it on the floor.

Nothing fit me anymore, but I was determined to squeeze into something I owned. And it had to be black.

Sweat was permeating my forehead when Rush walked right into the middle of my wardrobe crisis.

"What's going on in here?"

"I should've bought a new outfit for tonight. None of my old stuff fits me. I'm at that weird point where I'm not really showing, but I just look fat and don't fit into any of my clothes."

Looking good tonight was imperative because I was going to be meeting Rush's family. Granted, he didn't get along with them, but that didn't mean I didn't want to look good.

It surprised me when Rush had asked me to accompany him to his estranged brother's birthday party in the City. While I was curious to meet the bad apples—his father and brother—it made me really nervous. But he told me he'd promised his sister-in-law—the one I'd met at The Heights—that he would at least show up.

Rush had an extra collared shirt hanging around in my closet from one of the last times we'd gone out to a fancy restaurant. He took it down and said, "Humor me. Try on this shirt."

"Are you kidding me?"

"No. It needs to be pressed, but put it on for a minute. I have an idea."

Wrapping myself in the large black shirt, I laughed as I buttoned it up. It was actually long enough to wear as a dress but it was way too baggy.

Rush grabbed a thick, red patent belt that was hanging in my closet and placed it around my waist. He pushed up some of the material above the belt then rolled up my sleeves halfway and adjusted the collar.

I stood there speechless as he walked over to my jewelry box and grabbed a strand of pearls that had belonged to my father's mother. He lifted my hair up and fastened it around my neck.

He then led me over to the mirror that was affixed to the wall.

Rush placed his hands on my shoulders from behind. "What do you think?"

The ensemble actually looked really good. I couldn't believe he'd pulled this off—that this shirt could actually pass off as a dress and look stylish at that.

"I love it. It's perfect. And it doesn't make me feel fat at all. I would have never taken you for a fashionista."

"I'm not. I'm just good at thinking on my feet during times of crisis." He pointed to my shoes that were lined up on the closet floor. "Those red heels I love would go perfect with it, too."

Flipping around, I wrapped my arms around his neck. "You're like my hero tonight, you know that? I owe you big time later."

"I'm sure I'm gonna love taking this off even more than I loved putting it on."

———

Rush was strumming his fingers along the steering wheel during the car ride to the City. He definitely seemed tense, and that was understandable.

I placed my hand on his knee. "Are you sure you want to do this? We don't have to go. We could just go out to eat somewhere else."

"I told my brother's wife I would show up. She's been begging me for weeks. She's delusional, because she thinks that somehow my relationship with him can be repaired. I'm only doing this for her. She's always been nice to me. But honestly, a part of me wants to show up just to put a damper on his birthday because he's such a dick. So, there's that."

"We don't have to stay long if it's going to upset you to be around them."

"I'll be fine. I'm a big boy. I deal with them all of the time in business meetings. A couple of hours at a party isn't gonna kill me."

The fact that he wasn't smoking anymore wasn't lost on me.

"I want you to know that I am so proud of you for not lighting up right now, because I know you really want to. You would normally be smoking one after the other in a situation like this."

"Yeah. Let's not even mention cigarettes, okay?"

I cringed. "Sorry."

He glanced over at me. "Got any other ideas to relieve stress while I'm driving?"

"I would totally go down on you right now, you know. Don't tempt me."

"Nah. I won't let you take your seatbelt off, not with my precious cargo. I might let you give me head in the bathroom at my brother's house, though."

"Anything to make you feel better."

He cocked a brow. "You'll do *anything*, huh?"

"Pretty much."

"That's one of the things I love about you, beautiful."

Once in Manhattan, we parked near Rush's brother's place then walked a few blocks to the luxury building.

A doorman checked our names on a list and brought us to a private elevator that led right up to the penthouse suite.

As soon as the doors opened a wave of heat hit me as we entered the crowded room. Waiters passed around trays of hors d'oeuvres and champagne. The city lights lit up the space through the massive floor-to-ceiling windows. Someone was playing a grand piano at one end of the living room.

So many people were talking over each other, and that made everything sound muffled. I really wished I could have had a drink. Meeting new people always made me a bit nervous, but especially in this case, given the tension between Rush and his father and brother.

Rush went to fetch me a glass of water. He returned with one and a flute of champagne for himself.

The beautiful blonde woman I remembered from The Heights walked toward us with a big smile on her face. "Rush! I'm so glad you could make it."

She was wearing a long, black gown that seemed way too formal for a birthday party, even one as ritzy as this.

"Good to see you, Lauren," he said.

She turned to me. "Gia, right ? Nice to see you again." She flashed her pearly whites before giving me a quick once over. I wondered if she figured out that I was wearing Rush's shirt.

Lauren looked like she'd just gotten a fresh spray tan. It looked sparkly, like she had specks of glitter over her flawless skin. Her golden locks were done up in a twist.

"Nice to see you again, too." I smiled.

"Please partake in some appetizers and drinks. We have Elliot's favorite restaurant La Grenouille catering dinner later, so save some room."

Someone came by and swept her away into another conversation.

Turning to Rush, I asked, "Where's your brother?"

He downed the last of his champagne and surveyed the room. "I don't see him yet."

"Do you think he' s going to be an asshole to you?"

"No. He'll be fake and nice around other people. He'll be nice around you, too, because he flirts with any woman who's not his wife. He's mainly a dick to me when no one's watching." Rush kissed my forehead.

"You want me to grab you some pigs in a blanket or whatever the fuck they're passing around?"

"Nah. I'm good. Feeling a little queasy, actually. Not that hungry."

Rush grabbed a scallop wrapped in bacon off of one of the trays and popped it into his mouth.

I glanced around. "God, you can just smell the money, can't you?"

"And the bullshit, too." Rush looked toward the corner of the room. "Speaking of bullshit, there's Richie Rich over there—my brother."

When my eyes landed on the corner Rush was pointing to, my heart felt like it stopped for a moment. There were three men engaged in a conversation. The longer my eyes lingered on one of the guys, the more certain it became that I knew him.

He was wearing a bowtie.

With each passing second that I stared at his face, I became more and more nauseated.

I squinted, trying my best to see clearly—to be sure. *Oh God.*

My throat felt like it was closing.

I was pretty sure it was—Harlan.

Harlan who I was never supposed to see again.

Harlan who gave me the wrong number after our one-night stand.

Harlan who had gotten me pregnant.

Memories of that night flashed through my brain like a movie on rewind. I kept staring at his face. The same eyes. The same square jaw. The same way he parted his hair to the side. The same perfect white teeth. The same charming smile. That laugh.

It was him.

Oh my God! It's him!

My heart was pounding out of my chest, and it felt like the room was spinning.

I managed to get the words out. "Which...which one of those guys is your brother?"

Rush sucked on his toothpick, then pointed it over at him. "The one with the bowtie."

The End...

For now...

Rush and Gia's story continues in *Rebel Heart,* coming May 22, 2018

ACKNOWLEDGEMENTS

We are eternally grateful to all of the bloggers who enthusiastically spread the news about our books. Thank you for all of your hard work and for helping to introduce us to readers who may otherwise never have heard of us.

To Julie – Thank you for always being there. We are so lucky to have your friendship, daily support, and encouragement.

To Elaine – An amazing proofer, editor, formatter, and friend. Thank you for your attention to detail and for helping to make Rush and Gia the best that they could be.

To Luna – Our right-hand woman. You are incredibly talented, but more than that an incredible friend.

To Erika – Thank you for your friendship, love, and support. Your eagle eye is pretty awesome, too.

To Sommer – Your design for this cover was better than we could have conjured up in our imaginations. Thank you for capturing that rich look we love so much.

To Dani – Thank you for organizing this release and for always being just a click away when we need you.

To our agent, Kimberly Brower – We're so excited for the year ahead and are grateful that you will be there with us every step of the way. We are so lucky to call you a friend, as well as an agent.

Last but not least, to our readers – We keep writing because of your hunger for our stories. We love surprising you and hope you enjoyed this book as much as we did writing it. Thank you as always for your enthusiasm, love, and loyalty. We cherish you!

Much love,
Penelope and Vi

OTHER BOOKS BY VI KEELAND & PENELOPE WARD

Dear Bridget, I Want You

Mister Moneybags

Playboy Pilot

Stuck-Up Suit

Cocky Bastard

OTHER BOOKS BY
VI KEELAND

Standalone novels
Sex, Not Love
Beautiful Mistake
EgoManiac
Bossman
The Baller
First Thing I See

Life on Stage series (2 standalone books)
Beat
Throb

MMA Fighter series (3 standalone books)
Worth the Fight
Worth the Chance
Worth Forgiving

The Cole Series (2 book serial)
Belong to You
Made for You

YA/NA Novel
Left Behind

OTHER BOOKS BY PENELOPE WARD

Gentleman Nine

Drunk Dial

Mack Daddy

RoomHate

Stepbrother Dearest

Neighbor Dearest

Sins of Sevin

Jake Undone (Jake #1)

Jake Understood (Jake #2)

My Skylar

Gemini

Made in the USA
Monee, IL
03 May 2020

29422218R00171